Basic Magick

Basic Magick

A Practical Guide

Phillip Cooper

WeiserBooks
Boston, MA/York Beach, ME

First published in 1996 by
Red Wheel/Weiser, LLC
York Beach, ME
With offices at:
368 Congress Street
Boston, MA 02210
www.redwheelweiser.com

Library of Congress Cataloging-in-Publication Data
Cooper, Phillip.
Basic magick : a practical guide / Phillip Cooper.
p. cm.
Includes bibliographical references.
1. Magic. I. Title.
BF1611.C743 1996
133.4'3--dc20 95-53254
ISBN 0-87728-832-1 CIP
BJ

Typeset in 11 point Palatino
Printed in the United States of America

07 06 05 04 03 02
11 10 9 8 7 6 5

The paper used in this publication meets the minimum requirements of the American National Standard for Permanence of Paper for Printed Library Materials Z39.48–1984.

Table of Contents

Foreword

I firmly believe that Magick is a science; it is provable, logical, and offers solutions to questions that cannot be explained by existing dogma. In the days before the cataclysm, when the one god came to drive out the many gods, the great science was Magick, and Magick was very much part of life. Since those times we have had about two thousand years of presumption with occasional glimpses of the truth. Now it must change for the better for this is the dawning of the age of creativity.

Only when we adopt a scientific approach to Magick will we ever begin to glimpse the sheer power, rightness, and magnificence of cosmology. To do this we will have to change our viewpoint; we will have to question and move forward. Within ourselves, within our own minds, there is a part of us that yearns for truth, knowing that the truth will set us free and bring abundance into our lives. There is also a part of us which still listens to a legacy bequeathed to us of quaint and whimsical ideas about Magick that is based on outdated and absurd conceptions. Most magical practices adhere to dubious traditions that have little basis in truth even if they do appear to offer something better.

Let me give you my considered opinion as to the way in which Magick will change. Magick is a science and this will be realized; Magick will be both philosophical and pragmatic in every respect. New discoveries will be made of inestimable value to humankind, as mundane science allies with the greater science of Magick. Temples will be constructed in such a way as to enable esoteric thinkers to utilize natural forces in ways undreamed of today.

The study and practice of Magick will expand and extend consciousness, allowing us to explore other dimensions which begin within ourselves—in our subconscious mind. By exploring these dimensions, we may venture into the universal subconscious mind, that vast realm wherein the archetypal gods abide. Anything which can be used will be used, but more intelligently.

The futuristic temples will be filled with meaningful symbolism designed to attune the subconscious mind in the best possible way. Color, scent, and sound will also be used to great effect. Sound will be synthesized along precise channels and frequencies, again for maximum psychological effect, and this will be linked to color symbology which imitates the workings of the cosmos at any given time or place. The temple will become a tool for scientific research into the vast potential of the mind. There will, however, be an important difference in that these psychic laboratories will be filled with hope and will reverberate with life energies.

In my vision of the future, there is hope for humankind, because the one true science will once again serve us. People will be cured by natural means, no longer will there be the pain and misery of surgery, or the horrors of supposed wonder drugs. The human mind will cure our afflictions. The magical sciences will answer our questions, remove our doubts, and give us a purpose for living by revealing the truth. The one great science scorned, abused, and almost buried by ignorance will once again emerge to pave the way to reality. If this seems idealistic or fanciful, so be it. The power of the human mind is awesome, and the reward is as infinite as any man or woman may conceive—for whatsoever we envision eventually comes to pass. You must judge for yourself. If my hypothesis is correct, then surely the world will bring us truth and happiness, and is this to be casually brushed aside in the need to agree with everyone else who is thinking conditionally?

The alternative is to listen to the "no hope" philosophies of those who offer only karma, retribution, and endless forced rebirth. Be honest, would you rather have a dream or a recurring nightmare? It is your right to choose, and your right to dream; dreams are powerful images that affect the subconscious mind. Dreams come true. Should we really continue to fill our minds with dreams of destruction and total annihilation? Or can we better ourselves by dreaming of fulfillment? As change is inevitable, we must adapt and evolve. The future is not yet made—it can be whatever we desire. The future is ours, if we will only put aside outmoded concepts and use the techniques of scientific Magick instead.

Introduction

This book is divided into two parts. The first part is Principium Magikos—an exegesis of the art and science of Pragmatic Magick. Here I explain the pure theoretical underpinnings of Magick in order that novices, when ready to perform Magick, may know what they are doing and be at all times in control of the outcome. Principium Magikos provides step-by-step practical guidance to prepare for the exercise of Magick; it sets out instructions on how to create and perform rites that will have precisely the desired effect, and offers one complete ritual by way of illustration. This book teaches how and why Magick works in an easy to understand way, free from confusion, ridiculous ideas, and outmoded thinking that belongs to our best-forgotten past. It brings Magick out of the dark ages and into the computer age.

The second part is the Cosmonomicon, which details an explanation of the symbolism with which we communicate with our subconscious mind, and gives an exegesis of the use of planetary energies and cosmic forces. I present Magick as it is and as it should be: a science freed from charlatanism, dogma, and the mystic demagogue.

Although the contents of this book may be considered Cabbalistic in nature, the use of these techniques should appeal to all kinds of ritualists. Cabbalistic Magick appeals to those who are Hermetic in outlook. In other words, we use our minds to work Magick. The other side of the coin is Orphic, an emotional approach. The division is never as final as this, for any rite that works must have some emotional content if we are Hermetic, and must have some mental discipline if we are Orphic. Whatever system we follow, the same fourfold pattern is our basis, and we cannot be effective as magicians without understanding this pattern. This is the idea I have tried to provide in this book—a solid basis on which to work Magick. If properly pursued on monistic-subjective principles, the study and practice of Magick should become a simple and effective way to control our future by tapping the inexhaustible resources of the subconscious mind. This, in turn, will expand and extend our consciousness, thereby improving the intellect.

Part One

Principium Magikos

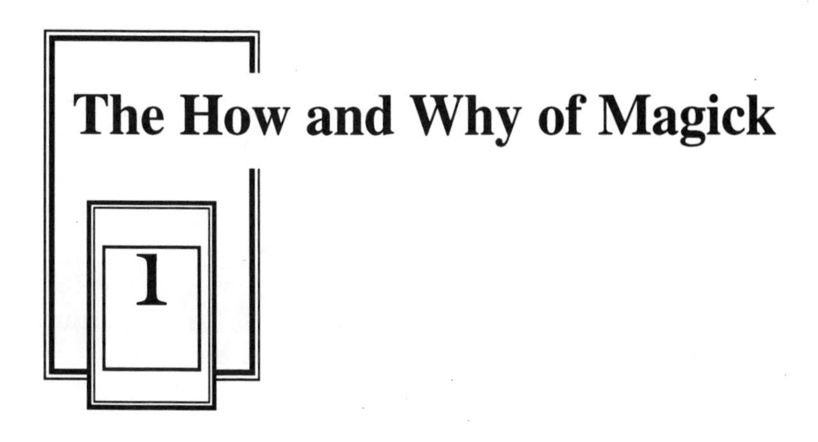

1 The How and Why of Magick

Welcome to this very special book of Pragmatic Magick, a book designed to help you understand what Magick is all about. I will show you how to change your life by using your inherent power in a safe and natural way. I want to present the truth about Magick and the magical way to success, no matter what the word "success" may mean to you. In acting as your guide, I am able to point the way to truth, for not only have I spent a lifetime searching for that rare commodity, I am not bound by oaths to keep silent. In any case, the truth about life is quite plain to see once the way has been cleared and the path pointed out. Perhaps we ought to start by looking at the analysis of "Truth."

If you are perfectly honest with yourself, truth is what you really want. I mean REAL TRUTH, and not the imperfect truths given to us by those who attempt to direct magical arts, both past and present. The biggest problem with most concepts is that they are based on secondhand knowledge. No one has bothered to think about or question ancient concepts.

The present magical revival has been underway for a decade, but there are still only a few practitioners who actually understand the subjective nature of Magick. Most contemporary magicians are naive about the true operative technique. The reason why so few get results is because only a few know the secrets.

Secondhand knowledge is no guarantee of success. That is one reason why the spells, incantations, and grimoires of others are not necessarily of any use to you. The only knowledge worth having is the truth, and once you have discovered this for yourself, you cannot fail.

There is a great deal of difference between accepted ideas which are made to work, and truth. Time and time again it can be proved that you can make anything work (and I do mean anything!) if you BELIEVE it to be true. Belief is a major key in life, and in Magick, for whatever you believe comes true. It makes sense to believe in the right ideas; in other words, those things which are true, as opposed to someone else's misconceptions, or their religious or philosophical beliefs. I will teach you to look for the real truth as it applies to you. I will teach you to question both your own beliefs and the accepted teachings of others and help you find the only path in life that matters—your own.

Truth Versus Untruth

If we are to establish what truth is, we had better start by looking at it from a different angle, by looking at some of the accepted "truths" that are held as being correct and absolute.

Ideas about "God"

As God is the source of all power, we have to beg and belittle ourselves to trust that God MAY hear us and grant some of our requests. Untrue. Our ideas about God are completely wrong, largely due to popular religion, and further suppositions on our part. There is a constant source of all-pervading energy which can be approached as "God." What matters is our METHOD of approach. A negative approach gets negative results, while a positive approach gets beneficial results every time. It is vitally important to remember that our image of God determines what we get from God.

What kind of god do you believe in? Do you believe in a god at all? Or do you, as many magically-minded people do, believe in many gods? The reason there are so many gods, or many different versions of God, is because each person will have a different point of view and will see God in different ways.

Fate and Predestiny

It is quite absurd to believe that we have no control over our lives; this is a misconception based on fixed irrational notions held stubbornly in the light of evidence to the contrary and, incidentally, a belief fostered by those who like to make money out of people's apparent misfortune.

What is true is that our beliefs control what happens to us. If those beliefs are negative, destructive, and self-limiting, we are bound to get effects which are in keeping with them, such as illness, poverty, stress, and bad luck. Being human, we have to blame something (or somebody). Naturally, we dare not blame God, or even consider that it may be our own fault, so we blame intangibles, such as forces beyond our control. It may seem like a valid idea but, as we will see, it is not. In truth, the only force which controls our lives is our own and this force acts through our beliefs.

Devils, Demons, and other Astral Entities

Like gods, these are images—components of the personality. Despite the unfounded ramblings of pseudo-magical practitioners, let me categorically state that, in reality, there are no such beings, and they certainly do not exist outside yourself. At this point, you may be experiencing something of a letdown. Am I saying that angels, demons, goddesses, and gods of old are only figments of the individual's imagination? Certainly not! The gods are real, and their power is awesome. Magical trances or altered states of consciousness are the key to entering their kingdom, the Olam Yetzirah, or the Astral Plane, of which more will be said later on. Images and visions of spirits are actually archetypes evoked from the deep-mind via magical trance, and are an important part of magical technique, especially the personal images, or visions, such as archangels, and so on. It all depends on what you are trying to achieve. If you are seeking to bring good into your life, you use beneficial images such as (realistic) gods and angels. If you are concerned with ridding yourself of unwanted evils, then you personify these as demons and such. These are advanced techniques best reserved for more advanced magical work. Unfortunately a little knowledge can often be a dangerous thing in the hands of fools who imitate, but do not fully understand, these images.

Instant Magick

Like anything else in life, the more you put in, the more you get out. There is no such thing as instant Magick, because the magical arts need study and practice. You can no more make these absurd ideas work than you can, say, pick up a French dictionary and expect to speak the language fluently.

Spells and Chants

There is a great deal of misunderstanding about these techniques. Words can be extremely powerful if they are understood. It is quite possible that the magician who first conceived the spell may well have made it work because he put a great deal of thought and feeling into the words—he gave the words power by belief. It does not follow that anyone else repeating those same words will get the same results because the words belong to someone else. The personal involvement is missing. You can literally chant away until you are blue in the face, but unless you work up some emotional fire and belief in what you are saying, nothing will ever happen. If you are ignorant of the value of ritual wording, you may delude yourself.

Joining a Lodge or Coven

It is quite natural for the would-be magician who has met with failure, confusion, or uncertainty to seek the company of those in the know. The more unscrupulous organizations will be more than pleased to show you inner secrets (for a price) and offer you initiation into these mysteries. What mysteries? The secrets of Magick are quite plain to see, and demand no loyalty to some cause or oaths of silence. Most of these lodge secrets can be found in books if you search about for them.

The only true way to personal power is by individual effort. Of course you can learn from others, but you must avoid the herd instinct that leads to joining magical organizations.

The Truth

The following statement of fact cannot be overstressed. The essential truth about life, particularly from an esoteric point of view, is as follows:

YOU = BELIEF = LIFE ENERGY

If you were expecting profound and mystical truths, complex formulae, or some tremendous revelation, you could be excused for being surprised. Centuries of muddled thinking have made life appear to be far more complex than it really is. Think long and hard about those three words. They are a master key to success, simple though they may appear.

Life Energy

Let us start by looking at creation in a simplified way. First creative intelligence (God) created life energy. This was then split into distinct categories in the same way that light can be divided into colors of the spectrum.

From a magical point of view, these became known as the planetary energies, of which more will be written later. However, energy by itself is not sufficient to produce the physical universe in which we live. There has to be something into which this energy can be directed. That "something" is known as matter. Matter is formless, shapeless, and inert. It is, for all intents and purposes, quite dead. Life is created when matter is given energy. The lifeless "nothing" becomes "some-thing." Everything that we see and touch is matter which contains energy—everything from a pebble to the human body. The essential difference between one object, such as a stone, and another, such as water, is the type of energy which it contains.

Magick is the art of getting to know about this energy and learning how to use it. Before we can do this, we have to look a little deeper.

Beliefs

Each and every one of you has the ability to create around yourself all that you wish to have. In fact, you are doing this right now! Before you start to write letters telling me all about your misfortunes, unhappiness, and lack of money, I urge you to think carefully about the absolute truth which follows.

There are many myths, mythoi, and profound statements which allude to our inherent power. Time after time, great teachers have pointed out the reality of our hidden abilities, yet very few have listened. The key to life is contained in the word "belief."

Suppose you owned a vast computer which was capable of answering any question and could also, through other computers, robots, and so forth, bring anything to your door. If you think about the rapid advances being made in technology, this is not as farfetched as you may suppose. All you have to do is ask your computer, and it does the rest without any further effort on your part. As a human being, you have such a device. It is called the subconscious mind. This incredible mental computer is capable of anything, and, furthermore, it can be directed by you, if you know how.

There are many techniques that attempt to influence the subconscious mind. Among these are hypnosis, alpha states, magical or ritual trance, autosuggestion, altered states of consciousness, and mind power. Correct magical procedure uses only the best techniques together with the only language which the subconscious mind can understand—symbols. As you will see, Magick without symbolism is quite pointless.

We will delve further into the mysteries of the subconscious in subsequent chapters. However, it is important to understand the part that belief plays in this matter. Always remember that beliefs are not restricted to religious issues; we have beliefs about everything.

Unfounded Beliefs

Each one of us has any number of blocks that prevent the effective use of power. These blocks may manifest as fears, phobias, compulsions, strange ideas, and beliefs or non-beliefs that we have accepted without thinking. Magick can only be totally effective when all these blocks are realized and replaced by truth! This truth is again different for each person, as we all have a different point of view and no two people see the same thing in the same way.

In olden days, these blocks were conceived as demons in the same way that angels represented the higher aspects. If you wish to use the visual image of a demon or an angel, then do so! However, keep in mind that they are only components of your personality, or serious error will result. These things are not real, and are not to be given any importance they do not warrant. The idea of bowing the knee to an angel, or fleeing from a demon is ridiculous! In the invocation of the so-called holy guardian angel, the lower self, undesirable blocks are made to prostrate themselves to the higher self. As long as this is borne in mind, all is well and good. The idea falls apart when the holy guardian angel is presumed to be remote, and the operator identifies with the lower self while assuming strange ideas of self-flagellation and unworthiness. This is a classic case of the demon winning on all points.

We are evolved! We have power! All we have to do is rediscover it. Tackle each block as you come to it. If something appears not to work, then there is a reason for this, and "God's will" is no longer a valid excuse.

Incorrect Presumption

Here we are dealing with largely unfounded beliefs which can be made to work. I will not go into detail; the never-ending list grows each day. However, it will suffice to say that incorrect presumptions have no place in real Magick. They do, however, play a major role in today's esoterics and are often not easy to identify. As an example, consider the concept of consecrating ritual implements. When fully understood, the act of consecration is a powerful magical act. Mumbling a few words together with assorted gestures over ritual implements is quite pointless because it is presumed by incorrect belief that the implements are, in themselves, magical. They are not; no ritual equipment is, in itself, magical.

Ritual equipment is only an aid to focusing the mind and nothing else. The golden rule with Magick is: Never do or say anything that you do not fully understand. When you understand something, you remove the chances of failure.

Positive Beliefs

When you exert positive belief, you ignore all the apparent facts while concentrating on that which is desired. This is the essence of most mind power books and it is totally correct. Always keep in mind that the old idea of seeing is believing is not necessarily true. The more you become involved with Magick, the more you will begin to realize that "facts" are not necessarily true. They only appear to be true. Real Magick ignores the facts, and concentrates, instead, on the goal, because it is realized that facts can be changed. I could list hundreds of cases in which the apparent facts have been pushed aside in favor of something better.

You

You are made in the image of God—so the Bible tells us. This is not a myth, it is absolute fact! You are the only creature on this planet who has the capacity to create using life energy. That which can be described as "God" creates a universe; you create within the universe according to your will. There are no limitations on the ability to create. You have, above all else, free choice.

Naturally, this is akin to a sword that cuts both ways. If you have negative beliefs, you get negative results. If you have positive beliefs, you get positive results. Free choice is being exercised because they are your beliefs, no matter where you got them from. By changing your beliefs, you change your life.

Your subconscious mind is a wonderful creative tool. Give it an instruction (in other words, a belief) and it will carry this out without any further action on your part, just like the computer previously mentioned. The art and science of instructing the subconscious mind in this way is called Magick, and this is the sole reason why magical techniques work. You, as an individual, can and will learn how to do this in the safest, most natural way. You already have power, and that power is probably leaking away, or being wasted on unrealistic beliefs such as poverty, illness, and lack.

There is no external cause for people's problems. The real cause lies within the subconscious mind. Even science is beginning to realize this fact, for many illnesses are being diagnosed as psychosomatic, in other words, as in the mind. If people's beliefs cause their troubles, where do they get them from? The answer is quite complex.

From the moment you are born, you are constantly being bombarded with impressions as you learn. It is scientific fact that the first few months of life tend to shape the character of the child. Children, particularly babies, are very receptive. If the impressions they receive are largely beneficial, they grow up well-balanced and optimistic because their beliefs are generally positive. If, on the other hand, the impressions received are restrictive and jaded, the result is negative belief patterns, which give rise to serious problems. If you look around, you will see the evidence of this in yourself and in others.

Once a person exercises the right of free choice and begins to question, things start to change almost at once. Any degree of serious thinking awakens the subconscious mind. If questions are being asked, it will immediately start to provide answers, for the subconscious mind always seeks to serve, just like the lamp of Aladdin. It responds to your desires.

Remember that no matter what has happened in the past, no matter what your belief patterns have done to your life, your subconscious mind is always there to help. It is your servant. From this point of view alone, your future is therefore always bright. No matter what lies behind you, success lies ahead, providing that you make the effort. To recapitulate:

1. There is abundant life energy freely available to you. No god or other religious entity measures this out in small doses in proportion to your worthiness. There is more than enough energy for everyone and it will never run out.

2. You have a subconscious mind which is your servant. It will do whatever you wish, using life energy to manifest your desires into physical fact. All you have to do is give it instructions. Magick is concerned with the giving of such instructions.

3. Beliefs are the key to magical power. It is most important to replace wrong beliefs with truth. Only by getting rid of outmoded and self-limiting beliefs can life take on a new meaning.

Turning Desires into Reality

Remember this magical rule: Input = Output. There is no such thing as instant Magick. Everything takes time. In order to get the most out of Magick, you will have to study the ideas I give in each chapter and then apply them. Do not skim through each chapter and then rush into the practical work; go slowly and steadily. Think carefully about all that has been written and try to understand the ideas given to you.

There is no substitute for patience, persistence, and regular daily study. The more you put in, the more you get out. This is true in life and certainly true in Magick. One of the greatest causes of failure is expecting something for nothing. If you want to change your life, become successful and content, then you must be prepared to work. This means that you will have to devote some time each day to your studies and practical work. It is a small sacrifice for a large gain.

A prerequisite for successful magical work is the ability to become calm. You cannot work effective rituals, and thereby influence your subconscious mind, if you are in a state of turmoil. This preliminary meditation serves as a vital transition stage between the mundane world and the sacred dimensions of the Inner Temple, of which more will be said later. In a temporal sense, it will lead you smoothly from real time into dream time. Learn to relax, especially before attempting a magical act or exercise. This is not difficult to do. All you have to do is breathe slowly and gently, and then let go of everyday thoughts. In a similar way, slowly work through your body, feeling it relax, little by little. Tension is the enemy of ritual because it blocks access to your subconscious mind.

The relaxation exercise can be performed sitting or lying down. From your toes gradually work up the body to the top of your head, relaxing each part as you come to it.

This exercise can be taken one stage further by standing upright with your arms at your sides, eyes open or closed. This exercise involves five central points on your body, and these points correspond to the five central spheres on the Cabbalistic Tree of Life. See figure 1 on page 16.

You will concentrate on each of the five areas (Kether, Daath, Tiphereth, Yesod, and Malkuth), one at a time beginning with the head, and as you do, endeavor to imagine a sphere of brilliance pulsating with the correct color energy. Spend a little time on this before moving to the next position. When the ankle area is reached, then return. Start at the ankles, and move back up the body toward the head to complete the cycle.

To reiterate, concentrate your whole mind upon the crown of the head; visualize a sphere of white brilliance. Concentrate on just that part of your body, as though it were the only part of you that was alive and active. After doing this for a minute, concentrate your attention upon your throat area; visualize a sphere of lavender-blue brilliance, feel your neck and skin, and the air flowing down it. When your consciousness has been centered in this part of your body, then bring the consciousness down to your heart area; visualize a sphere of yellow brilliance; feel the flesh and the internal organs of this area, feel your heart beating. Become conscious of your lungs and the rhythm of breathing.

Now bring your consciousness down further until you reach your lower stomach, the genital area; visualize a sphere of violet brilliance. Become aware of the internal workings and feel of this area.

Finally, concentrate your attention upon your ankles and feet, visualizing a sphere of brown or green brilliance. Feel your consciousness in your feet and heels, the existence of your toes. Now reverse this process, starting at your feet-ankle area, and gradually work back up through each area, finishing at the crown of your head once more.

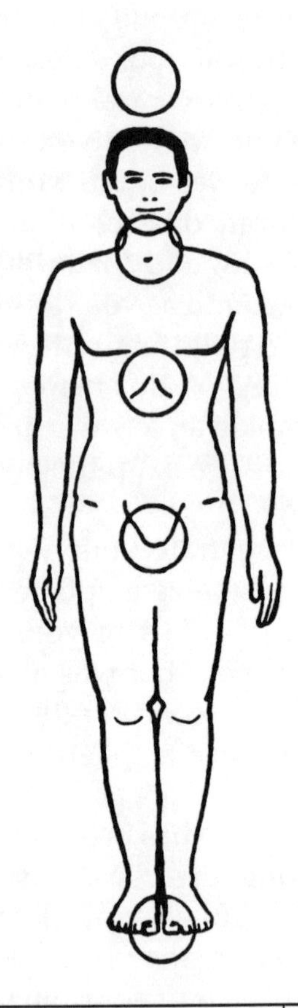

Kether	(Uranus)	Crown of Head	Color: White
Daath	(Pluto)	Nape of Neck, Throat	Color: Lavendar-Blue
Tiphereth	(Sun)	Heart	Color: Yellow
Yesod	(Moon)	Genitals	Color: Violet
Malkuth	(Earth)	Ankles, Feet	Color: Brown or Green

Figure 1. Quickening the subconscious.

The point of this exercise is to gradually concentrate and awaken a consciousness in each area of the body. This will cause the blood to be excited in those parts. It will cause the objective consciousness, as well as the subjective consciousness, to develop and increase in that part of the body. The nerve centers in those parts will be awakened by this process until, by the time you have reached the feet and returned back up to the head again, you will find that your whole body is tingling with life and vitality.

After having done this for three or four days, the next time you do it, take a deep breath and hold it while you concentrate on each of the five areas of the body. For instance, when you come to the crown of the head, take a deep breath through the mouth, hold it for half a minute; concentrate on this, visualizing (imagining and feeling) the sphere of brilliance, then exhale through the mouth. Then move down to the next position and do the same thing, only modifying the color of the sphere to suit the correct area. Each time, hold the deep breath that you have inhaled through the mouth while concentrating, then exhale and breathe out through the mouth.

You will find that this adds to your vitality. The deep breath gives you an extra amount of positive energy, which further quickens and enlivens the psychic senses of those parts on which you are concentrating. The extra amount of vitality that enters the blood cells of the lungs each time you take a deep breath and hold it is passed off by the blood in its circulation at the points where you are concentrating. You are feeding each of these points with an extra amount of vital life force which includes the very essence of physical and mental power that is required to awaken the psychic centers of those parts.

The Breath Mantram

By deep breathing, I mean inhaling (breathing in), but not to the point of discomfort. Then, hold the breath as long as possible, also without discomfort, and exhale as instructed. The use of a breath mantram will help concentration while visualizing each sphere of brilliance. The SU HAAM mantram can be put to good effect. The SU sound is made on the in-breath and the HAA sound is made on the out-breath, the M at the end of HAAM is made by closing the mouth. If you have a respiratory illness—such as a lung or heart ailment—I would advise dispensing with the deep breathing method. It is a good idea to use some soft music or slow drumming, and perhaps some joss sticks or general incense.[1] When you have absorbed the imagined light of the Cabbalistic sphere (or psychic center), and when this experience reaches its peak, move into the temple area or place of work, still maintaining your "set" or trance, ready for your magical work.

Ritual Bath

Even though it is not essential that you physically bathe or wash before a ritual, a physical action can serve to instigate a mental attitude. In Magick, it is essential that the mind be clear of all but the intention. The Magick is done on a subconscious level, and the reasoning logical mind, cluttered and clouded as it is by everyday events, invariably gets in the way. This is where the cleaning process is useful. A physical bath washes away the cares, troubles, and tensions of mundane living and leaves us calm, with a clear channel to the subconscious mind. This can also be achieved by a few moments of silent meditation; and, in-

---

[1]A joss stick is a small stick of incense burned in a Chinese temple.

deed, a physical bath should always be followed by a period of silence before any ritual is attempted. A physical bath can be dispensed with, but the silent mind part is essential. Unless the intent is carried through to the subconscious levels, all Magick will fail. Bathing, robes, candles, oils, and incense are only means of intensifying the subconscious will. To use a modern cliché, "They hammer home the message and get the point across."

An adept of many years training and control can dispense with the outward tools of Magick, for he or she has learned to control the many levels of the mind by a mental cleansing process. If you find that a bath helps, then use it. In fact, use whatever will bring about the desired state of consciousness.

Decide What You Want

Now we will do a really practical exercise of the utmost value. We all tend to think that we know what we want, but do we? You are about to find out. The best way to sum up magical procedure is:

THINK—ACT—FORGET

It is essential to think and plan out any magical ritual before you perform it. Thinking about your ritual intention helps get the intention firmly in the mind, and also helps you tackle any negative thoughts that will prevent success.

I want you to decide exactly what you want from life. Think about this carefully, and write down everything on a sheet of paper. While doing this, it is important that you not restrict yourself in any way. One way of doing this is to imagine that you have a limitless supply of blank checks and unlimited funds in the bank. Think about this. If you really did have an endless supply of money, what would you buy, where would you go, and so forth? Let your imagination run free, and watch out for any negative ideas, such as, "I cannot have that because of . . ." or similar ideas.

Another way to look at this is to pretend you have a Genie in a bottle, or even Aladdin's lamp. Use any ideas that help widen your horizons and give you unlimited free choice. Take your time and let everything come out into the open. When you are satisfied that you have covered everything that you need, take another sheet and divide this list into two sections—needs and desires.

There is quite a difference between something needed and something desired. For instance: if your health is bad, you need better health. A new car or a trip abroad could well be a desire. Again, take your time and think carefully about all this.

Finally, I want you to look at each of these two lists and put them in order of priority. The net result is that you are now clear in your mind as to exactly what you want from life, and you can also see which of these things are most important.

Spend some time on these exercises until you have become proficient; before moving on, take your time. Do remember to be positive. In other words, include everything no matter how impossible it may appear to be. In the next chapter, I will show you how to begin to turn these needs and desires into reality.

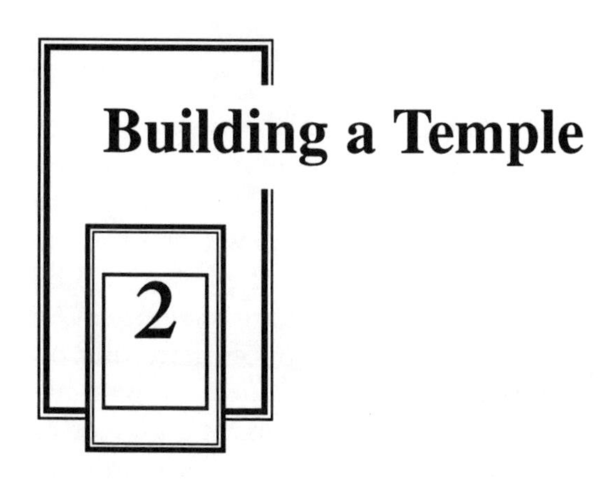

Building a Temple

2

There are some pretty idiotic ideas about magical temples. Most center around the idea that these are holy places in which certain divine (or unsavory) entities gather at the whims of the magician. This being the central theme, all else gathers around it. There is a magical law which states that if the center is wrong, then all else is wrong. So it is with temples. If the temple is conceived and constructed around the wrong ideal then the result is a shambles. Before looking at the temple we must, of necessity, look at the ideal around which it is to be built.

A Magick Temple

The sole function of a temple is to provide a controlled environment for magical work because the temple is nothing more or less than a workroom, albeit a special workroom. As Magick is a science of using the mind, it naturally follows that anything likely to affect the mind adversely should be excluded. Conversely, anything likely to enhance the mind is included. Let us start by looking at the exclusion of undesirable elements.

There are two areas to be considered: physical and nonphysical. Often these combine to produce problems, so the distinction is not exact. Of prime importance is security; in other words, the ability to prevent intrusion by unwanted individuals. A strong lock on the door, together with heavy curtains over the windows, serves to reduce the possibilities of distraction, but more to the point, they help promote peace of mind. The more peaceful you are, and the more relaxed and comfortable you feel, the better will be your state of mind. Naturally, the results are therefore more assured because you cannot hope to concentrate fully on what you are doing if half your mind is concerned with the possibility of distractions. Often, when sharing a place of residence with non-sympathizers, there are additional security problems, such as how does one carry on magical work without raising suspicions? There are no hard and fast rules as situations vary tremendously from person to person; however, a little thought and ingenuity will often solve the problem. Suitable cover stories such as yoga, meditation, and so forth, are one avenue worth exploring. Always remember that the more relaxed you are the better the result, so it naturally follows that time spent on sorting out these problems is well spent in the long run. Noise is another problem. This may be alleviated by using background music, drumming, or special narratives, but eventually you will train yourself to turn off to such things.

Having looked at some problems needing exclusion, let us now look at the temple setup. Temples vary according to available space, type of work being undertaken, and other more personal factors. The description which follows is of an ideal temple using universal symbolism equating to all realistic magical practices. We will discuss less adequate situations later. However, the same basics apply regardless of space or expenditure.

The Room

The first consideration is one of orientation. You may have read in some book that it is vital to align the temple to the points of the compass in order to captivate natural magnetic currents. This is not strictly true. You can work just as well without being aligned to magnetic north for most work, so this is not a major consideration. Only when magical work reaches a certain stage of development (for example: the deeper modes of Esoteric Magick), will it be found desirable to equate the temple to such lines of natural power. Until then you can manage quite well without.

Obviously, the four walls of the temple will have to be designated according to the elements and cardinal points. Here we have a choice either to be purely practical or to be in some reasonable alignment. Some examples will serve to illustrate this. We will presume that the designated temple is rectangular. This is ideal for practical considerations. It provides alignment and there is adequate space available in the center of each wall for stands, altar, and so forth. An ideal setup would have the altar in the center, rather than against a wall. Apart from the fact that this is symbolically correct (power emanates from the center), it also gives the advantage of allowing one to work toward any magical direction, as in seasonal work, or work with one's personal ruling planets. Although it is customary to work toward the east, this is a remnant of Judaic thought and plays no part in serious magical work. If the altar needs to be placed against a wall then any convenient wall will do. Then again, the altar placement could be left entirely to personal choice. Having looked at the room, let us now consider the equipment.

Equipment

Much depends on what kind of magical work you have in mind, but there are certain basics. Now let us forget all the mumbo jumbo about purifying or consecrating magical equipment. Most of the ideas are quite silly, being motivated by quixotic medieval conceptions rather than science. The whole point of magical equipment is simply to aid concentration of the mind—that is all. The important thing to remember is that magical equipment only becomes useful when a *relationship* is forged between magician and object. For instance, if you rush out and buy a Magick Sword, then expect it to work miracles by helping you command spirits or make the floor burst open and spill forth the legions of hell in cinemascope and stereophonic sound, you will either be bitterly disappointed, or you will forever delude yourself. If you consecrate the Sword, either with a ready-made ritual, or with one you have thought up yourself, you may improve matters slightly. Much depends on your powers of belief, however. There are two mistakes here: firstly that of presuming that the words of someone else will work for you and secondly, that of adhering to pseudo-magical concepts. Obviously this is not very satisfactory either. So what is the best approach? With all magical equipment, first ask the simple question: Do I really need this?

It is so very easy to spend a small fortune on equipment presuming that this is essential and that in some way it enhances your magical work. It may enhance your magical work if understood and used intelligently, but then again it may not.

Why do you need a robe? Because the book tells you so, or because it is essential? The truth is that you do not need a robe. Look at it this way: if the wearing of a robe makes you feel more at ease, more comfortable, then you have the right attitude of mind. If not, then do not bother. The whole idea is to help you change your attitude of mind from the mundane to the magical, and the changing of one's clothes helps this. Think of it this way: when you are going somewhere special you dress up to suit the occasion, which of course makes you feel better. You fit in with the situation. Clothes help create the right feel and mood. Consider the idea of going to some splendid function in sweater and worn-out jeans. You would feel out of place, uncomfortable and ill at ease. You would not just throw on any old thing, either, you would spend time thinking about what to wear and might even buy something special for the occasion. So it is with robes; if they make you feel good, then use them. Also remember the idea of choosing clothes for a special occasion and apply the same idea to robes. The more thought you put into this the better, which brings me to the next important point.

Equipment is Only as Good as You Make It

As mentioned, the relationship between you and your equipment is what really matters. How can you possibly have a relationship with a piece of equipment, I hear you say? Quite easy, whatever you come into contact with, be this persons or things, you automatically form a relationship by virtue of your attitude of mind toward them. Now, in magical work, attitude of mind is of paramount importance. We are, after all, dealing with the powers of the mind. The more personal contact between you and the object you intend to use, the better the result. This is one reason why magical practitioners are encouraged to make their own equipment whenever possible. The making of some ritual object helps forge this link because the magician will be putting his or her own thoughts and actions into practice. The end product is personal and is the result of using the magician's ingenuity and imagination. Now, obviously, not everyone can seriously consider making a Magick Sword out of a bar of steel. This requires considerable skill, not to mention the cost of the equipment needed to produce it, so unless you have the ability and the money, this is out of the question. So where do we go from here? Well, this is where the concept of ritual consecration came from. The idea is one of personalizing the object in question, of forming a special relationship with it. Other ideas have also been used, such as the inscribing of sigils and mottos, all designed to make the object special in a personal sense. There are many ways of doing this and the practice is quite valid providing the magician understands what he or she is really trying to do.

Overall, there are four points to remember when dealing with ritual equipment. These are:

1. What function does it have in Magick; in other words, what does it do?
2. In the light of this, is it really necessary to my work?
3. How can I make better use of it by personalization techniques?
4. Where applicable, is it symbolic?

Now let us look at some basic equipment.

The Altar

In line with the above points, first we must ask what is an altar and what does it do? An altar, as such, is not some holy object, it is simply a work surface, and to be perfectly frank, is no different from, say, a woodworker's bench. After all, you would find it highly uncomfortable trying to perform a ritual on the floor, so you need something convenient on which you can place candles, symbols, and so forth. That is the basic function of an altar. Now it really does not matter a hoot what shape or size this is, let personal choice be the judge. You can use whatever comes to hand, such as a cupboard or even a coffee table, or you can make one yourself. With regard to personalization, obviously a plain cupboard is hardly likely to be an inspiring sight and to all intents and purposes, it still is an ordinary cupboard. So, what to do? Think about this: use your imagination rather than copy ideas from other people. One useful idea is that of using an altar cloth. Not only does it help disguise the cupboard, it also gives you the opportunity to use color. Color is a superb way of enhancing rituals by giving the mind visual stimuli. Use it whenever possible. Traditionalists may opt for the double cube shape as this contains much in the way of symbolism. This can easily be made from chipboard or plywood, fastened together with screws and glue, then placed one on top of the other. The size can be eighteen inches by eighteen inches square. Paint the top cube white and the bottom cube black, castors can be attached to the bottom to make movement easier.

This, of course, brings us to the idea of symbolism so important in magical work. By varying the altar cloth's color to suit the type of energy being used, we can more easily attain contact with the power in question. Color symbolizes, or represents, a type of energy, usually planetary, although there are other types. For instance, red belongs to Mars, green to Venus, silver to the Moon, and so forth. The impact is immediate because the color suggests the appropriate energy.

Quarter Lights

These are important symbolic points which fit on to the Magick Circle. If you happen to have a floor design, well and good; if not, it does not really matter. There are certain advantages in having quarter stands, and these can be made quite easily out of wood and painted in the correct colors of the elements. As each elemental doorway is declared open, this may be symbolized by lighting the appropriate candle or lamp and extinguishing the appropriate candle or lamp upon closing the doorway. This becomes very effective with practice. If you do not have quarter stands at this present time, candleholders containing candles may be placed on the floor surrounding your altar at the cardinal points or on the altar itself.[1]

The Pillars

These are not essential in most work of a practical nature, but they do find a useful place in Esoteric Magick. Pillars have many uses. They may be used as a symbolic doorway through which we pass into the Inner Temple, or to the otherworld state, or as a doorway through which power flows into the temple, to name but three. They may be made from wood or even plastic pipe. The ideal colors are white to represent positive forces and black to represent receptivity. Candles or lamps may be placed on the tops. As a visual aid they are quite impressive and once again work far better if thought about carefully.

The Weapons

Again these find usage mainly in esoteric matters, but can be used in Pragmatic Magick if understood. There are four weapons to be considered.

The Sword. The ideas perpetuated by pseudo-practitioners are to be ignored. A Magick Sword is not used to prod demons out of the circle, or to command various entities to do your bidding. This is medieval quixotism, nothing more. The Sword is a symbol. It represents the element Air and equates to the eastern quarter. Used properly, it helps us direct and control this element. Once again apply the

---

[1]Make sure that all fire precautions are attended to; perhaps you can have a small fire extinguisher or fire blanket kept in some inconspicuous place.

rules given. Let us presume that you understand its function and have decided that you do need a Sword. Before you buy one of the more usual designs, which of necessity carry with them an assortment of outmoded and often incorrect concepts, stop and think. Use your imagination to determine the design that suits you. The more you think, the better will be your impressions of what this is to be in terms of design. By doing this you know which Sword is right for you, because you have brought this design out of your own subconscious. It is therefore yours. Having done this, you may then have one made to your own specifications, or may choose to modify the Sword nearest to your ideal. Again, the more you put into the final product the better it will serve you.

The Wand, Rod, or Spear. These are easily made with a minimum of skill. They may be made from ordinary wooden dowels or taken from a tree at some special time. The choice is yours again, bearing in mind the essential idea of thinking about this in order to ensure that it is truly personal. Symbolically, the Rod acts as control symbol for the element Fire and correctly equates to magical south.

The Cup or Chalice. This belongs to the element Water and equates to magical west. It need not cost a fortune or be made out of gold or silver. Let your own choice guide you after due consideration.

The Shield. This controls the element Earth and belongs to magical north. Like all the elemental weapons, the Shield should be thought about before being made. The size ought to be reasonable—at least twelve inches in diameter (eighteen inches is better). It can be made from plywood or even stiff cardboard, with a painted design on one side. The design is important and is again a question of choice. Do not just paint a Pentagram because this is supposed to be powerful. The design must be understood. It is symbolic. Try an Encircled Cross instead. The whole idea of the Shield is to present a concept of power or cosmic symbology, rather like a circuit diagram which gives masses of information to those who can read it. In part, the Shield is something that you contemplate and meditate on, so the design should be meaningful and should stimulate the imagination along the right lines. To this end, Shield designs may be subject to constant variation.

Additional Equipment

This is largely a matter of choice, but basic requirements would include anything likely to enhance your ritual work. An incense burner, together with a range of incense to cover all your requirements, is always desirable. The whole subject of incense is a confusing one, and different people advocate different concoctions. The study and compounding of incense is a highly specialized subject, and a branch of Magick which requires deep knowledge, devotion, and a feel for this vocation. With Magick, numerous problems have arisen because of wrong thinking perpetuated down the ages, and so it is with all acknowledged branches of the art. Incense was born from our ability to use the sense of smell to a higher degree than the animals, and through this it was learned not only which scent was associated with a physical object, but magical practitioners were also able to classify all physical objects by placing them under the rulership of the elements, planets, and signs. It is from this correct classification, or doctrine of correspondences, that the recipes for correct incense are drawn.

Without going into too much detail, if you wish to contact natural forces through their true physical line, it is essential that you use the correct incense for your rites. The mind associates with scent very quickly, and this is most useful in reverse, as the scent then brings the object to mind and, with practice, the power that is behind it. Incense also helps still the mind and create a tranquil atmosphere. A good alternative is to use incense sticks (joss sticks) as these are cheap and burn for long periods. Their disadvantage is that the range of scent is limited. In any case, always try to make your own incense according to correct recipes or buy it from a reputable supplier who has studied the subject.

The use of the cassette recorder is also recommended. This need not be an expensive setup, the cheaper machines are perfectly adequate. Cassette tapes give you the opportunity to bring sound and music into the temple, adding greatly to the impact of the ritual.

Temple Lighting

This needs special consideration. Do not just rely on ordinary electric light, as so much opportunity is then missed. Candles produce a natural, gentle light which is ideal for magical work and, of course, they may be obtained in many colors to suit whatever you have in mind. The ideal setup would consist of:

1. A central light, usually placed on the altar, to symbolize one's inner contact with power. A gold or white candle is ideal for this.
2. Four candles to represent the elements. These are colored: yellow for Air and east, red for Fire and south, blue for Water and west, green for Earth and north. These should ideally be placed on the four quarter stands, or failing this, upon the altar.
3. A range of candles to represent the type of energies you are working with. Usually these are the planets, the elements, and/or the spheres. For instance, if you were working with the energy of Mars, then a red candle would be used, red being the correct color correspondence for Mars. For more complex work, such as medi-

tations on the paths of the Tree of Life, it is possible to use candles as additional visual impact. For instance, suppose you were working path twenty-one from Chesed to Netzach. Use two candles, a blue one to symbolize Chesed and a green one to symbolize Netzach. A more complex version would involve a third candle to symbolize the path itself. This could be plain white, as it is not always possible to obtain exact path colors. Each candle is lit after the appropriate invocation.

The shape and size of candles is not important. Choose according to personal needs. I am often asked if it is necessary to allow a candle to burn away completely. The answer is no. Candles may be reused as often as you like, unless you have a particular reason for allowing them to burn away in one go. There are many magical aids in terms of physical symbols, and, naturally, the subject of temples could be discussed in far more depth, but it is hoped that sufficient basic information has been given to enable each student to decide what is best in the light of reality and to help with the task of setting up the temple.

Building an Inner Temple

The Inner Temple is a magical tool used to contact subconscious power. Your subconscious mind responds to imagery (pictures) and symbols—the Inner Temple is a perfect blend of these two principles. Building an Inner Temple is quite easy, given a little time it will help to build itself. The Inner Temple is a very special place holding many secrets. This temple is built within the mind of the magician. Whatever you build in your mind does exist, perhaps not in a physical sense, but exist it most certainly does. This is your very own temple of the mind, your inner kingdom. Remember those famous words: "But rather seek ye the kingdom of God; and all these things shall be added unto you."[2] Find the kingdom first, then you will have whatever you wish. Where is this kingdom? The kingdom of God lies within, within your own mind. You will discover this inner kingdom, and simply by using your imagination you may enter this kingdom whenever you wish.

The Kingdom of God

God or the kingdom are not separated from you, nor are they unobtainable. The kingdom of God lies within you: "Neither shall they say, Lo here! or, lo there! for, behold, the kingdom of God is within you" (Luke 17:21). It is your INNER MIND. How can you be separated from part of yourself? How can this be removed from you? It is not possible. Only wrong ideas, attitudes of mind, and incorrect beliefs appear to separate you, but in truth, you cannot be separated from that which is part of yourself. You have this inner kingdom, you have creative power: "Jesus answered them, Is it not written in your law, I said, Ye are gods?" (John 10:34). Accept this simple truth; let it work for you and allow this into your mind.

You and God are the Same

God lies within! Not in some far distant part of the galaxy or in some idealistic heaven, the God within is your inner mind. Therefore you and God are the same, you have the capacity to create, you are Godlike. If you would discover the limitless potential that you truly have, then you must follow the path of peace leading to inner-mind awareness. Your inner mind will listen, it will advise, it will protect, and it will create for you. But you must communicate in peace, for only in peace and tranquillity will your inner mind be able to assist you.

---

[2]Luke 12:31. This, and all following biblical quotes, are from the authorized King James Version of the Bible.

A Universe within You

You have only to enter this temple and ask. It is your right to know and your right to ask, for this place is yours and all that belongs in this place. Do not make the mistake of presuming that this is a childish game, or doubt the existence of this land and this temple. Your Inner Temple may not be made of solid stone, but it is made of something far more lasting—pure thought. The key to all mysteries is thought, for that which exists in the mind affects your earthly life. Many are those who do not know of their own Inner Temples; there are magicians who would give their right arm to discover what you now have and are learning, but sadly they are blind to the truth, seeking answers in the material world rather than in their own minds. You are discovering the seat of power and the realm of truth, cherish this, accept its simplicity, and you will never regret it.

This is a kingdom of pure thought in which you will find peace of mind, indulge in pure fantasy, or cause changes in the physical world. It is yours, your kingdom, your realm, your inner world. You must therefore control and rule as would a king or queen, you are a god in your own universe, and may be whatever you will to be, for whatever reason. The more familiar you are with the Inner Temple, the better will be the results, and the quicker will be the results in practical terms.

The Secret Temple of the Mind

You will extend the ideas given to you in chapter 1 and use the principles given in this chapter. The use of the Inner Temple will increase your contact with power.

1. Go into your temple or place that you have set aside for magical work. Sit down and relax; let all thoughts of the outside world leave you just for a while.

2. It helps if you have some incense sticks or general incense burning. Meditation music, or slow drumming, as a background will be found useful. After a little while, switch off any lights and light your central lamp or candle.
3. While you are doing this, realize that this light is symbolic. It represents your inner power. Contemplate this for a while, then perform the magical exercise.
4. When the exercise is finished, gently blow out the candle and leave the temple. Have a notebook which you can use as a "Book of Results." Write up any impressions—just short notes. Do this exercise once a day until you have become proficient at it.

The Inner Temple Exercise

Just imagine you see in front of you an Encircled Cross; move toward this symbol in your imagination. You see that this symbol is emblazoned on a door. Move toward this door and touch it. The door opens, revealing an Inner Temple.

The temple is quite dark inside, apart from a single light suspended from the ceiling in the shape of a crown. You are in a large square room. On the floor there are intricate designs which seem to be woven around an Encircled Cross. Right in the center underneath the light, set in the floor, is a circular pool filled with water. Set in the middle of each wall is an archway and door. These are colored; the one in front of you is yellow (east), the one on your right is red (south), the one behind you is blue (west), and the one to your left is green (north). You move toward the yellow arch. Floating in the air in front of the door, point up, is a Sword. Look at this Sword and study it well, for it is yours. Something is engraved on the blade, can you see what it says? Move toward the red archway. Inside the arch, floating in front of the door, is a Spear. Once again there is something engraved on the shaft. Now move on to the blue archway, where you will find a Chalice. There it is; look at it, and study the engraving on it. What does it say? Finally, move to the green archway. Inside, in front of the door, there is a Shield. It has a very simple yet special design on it. Remember this, for it is your personal design. There is also something engraved on this Shield. Can you see it?

Now go back to the pool in the center of the temple. This is a Magick Pool. The water is not really water; it is power and energy. Later on you will learn how to use this. It does have one other use, however; just like a crystal ball, it can be used to see into the future. Look into its depths, and it will tell you things and give you answers to questions. Look into the depths and allow images to come into your mind. (If you like, you can use some meditation music or slow drumming and have this playing throughout the exercise period.) Spend as long as you like meditating at the pool. A good period is about five minutes. When the exercise comes to an end, there is no need to go the long way back. This is a magical land. Right in front of you there is a door, just walk toward it and you are back in your own room in your own time once more.

Before you forget any important points, write these down in your notebook; one day they will come in very useful. Always remember you can enter this magical temple any time you wish. Eventually you will make the journey in a few seconds.

The Magical Self

3

In this chapter you will learn how to build a bridge between yourself and the infinite source of power. Although this may sound like a sweeping statement, it is not. It is perfectly feasible; in fact, this bridge already exists, and needs only to be recognized once more. Let us start by looking at the truth about life.

The Cosmic Paradigm

I cannot stress the importance of the following truth too strongly:

You = Beliefs = Life Energy.

This formula is the foundation on which life is built and it is a major key which unlocks the doorway to power.

You

You are a totally creative being. Nothing happens by chance, fate, or luck; everything in your life exists by virtue of the fact that you thought these things into existence. Before you start to counter this by pointing out obvious facts, such as that you lost your job, or fell ill through no fault of your own, and that you would never deliberately bring this sort of thing upon yourself, stop and read on.

You have access to unlimited power and total free choice in the way in which you use this power. This, of course, applies to everyone else, and has an important bearing on achieving successful results when dealing with other people. So why do things go wrong? Why is there so much illness, strife, and lack in life? The answer is quite easy to see if you take the time and trouble to consider the ideas given in this book.

Beliefs

The cosmic paradigm is perfect. It cannot be anything less, and it gives to each person, without exception, what he or she asks of it. Now think carefully. What have you asked of life and how did you ask? By asking, you open up a channel through which that which you desire can come into being. If, say, you ask a friend for the loan of "something," you are in fact creating a channel between the other person and yourself. From then on, it is all a question of choice. Your friend may or may not lend you the item in question. He or she has a choice. This is perfectly reasonable in human affairs; however, we mistakenly carry this idea of choice into our dealings with the infinite. That which is God (the infinite, the all-powerful, the source—call it whatever you wish), will never, in any circumstances, say no. It is vitally important that you realize and accept this profound truth. You have free choice—God simply obliges. Now, if God never refuses, why is it you do not receive what you want when you ask of God? The answer is simply that the way in which you ask always dictates what you get in return. Put another way, your beliefs, at the time of asking, actually get in the way and prevent success.

When you apply "if" to something, you automatically imply the possibility of failure. God and failure cannot coexist. Ask yourself, can the supreme intelligence who created this vast, marvellous universe, ever be accused of failure? The answer must be an emphatic no! The universe is perfect, the only imperfections are those created by human beings.

Any magical ritual is, in essence, a way of asking the intelligence behind life to supply our needs. This asking must be realistic: in other words, direct to the point with no "ifs" and "buts." By asking, you are constructing a belief pattern, and you therefore receive in accordance with those beliefs. Look at the way in which you ask of life, because the quality of this asking is proportional to the end results.

When you perform a magical ritual, a creative thinking exercise, or even a prayer for help, do you hope and wish that some distant entity may hear and then perhaps help if you are "lucky?" Look at this approach; it is totally negative and includes numerous "ifs." It cannot hope to be effective. You are not believing that you are bound to succeed, based on the knowledge that the infinite source will always supply, instead you are believing the reverse. The maxim must always be: when you ask, always presume that infinite intelligence will supply. By doing this, you are providing a necessary channel through which energy flows to achieve the results you desire.

The Facts

It will always be argued that "facts" speak for themselves. They cannot be refuted and certain facts are unalterable. This is nonsense, and I am here to tell you that the facts can be altered. This, after all, is what Magick is really all about! When you perform a magical act, what else are you trying to alter but the apparent facts! In reality, facts are transient rather than stable, like our ability to believe. Whatever you do, always remember that the infinite source of power (who created "fact") is quite prepared to help you alter these facts at your request. All you have to do is ask and then provide a channel of belief through which this may work. An example:

Fact: "I have no money." Why? "Just bad luck." (Remember that there is no such thing as "bad luck"—what is, in fact, wrong is a deep-rooted belief which is now producing lack.)

Result: There is now a choice. You could stay poverty-stricken, and keep on dealing in "facts." For example, you could borrow money, live on state aid, and so forth. Or, you could ignore the "facts" and ask of life instead. What you must do is change your beliefs and connect to abundant power by opening up a channel. This can be done at any time, with or without a full-scale magical ritual. Once you have decided to do this, you hold fast to this belief while ignoring the apparent facts. Results are then guaranteed. Surely this is better than accepting fate or bad luck?

Never let the supposed facts dictate how you must run your life, and never allow the facts to become the basis for belief. If you do, you are effectively throwing away your right to free choice and your entitlement to success.

In our example, it would be easy to believe the so-called facts and continue to presume that a shortage of money had to be accepted as the way of things. However, there is always a choice: either continue to allow the apparent facts to dictate how you must live, or be realistic by changing belief patterns, thereby allowing life energy to change the facts to your advantage. You can see examples of this all the time if you care to look. They vary from rags-to-riches stories to miracle cures. Look around and you will see evidence of how changed beliefs have changed the "facts."

Life Energy

Life energy is all-pervading; it is abundant; it is never-ending, and it is freely available. So far, we have you at one end of the equation, life energy and the intelligence behind this at the other end. Between the two we have beliefs. This equation is perfect; however, we need to look a little deeper if we are to make full use of it and so we must now look at the workings of the mind; in particular, the subconscious mind.

The Subconscious Mind

So far, I have discussed power, the intelligence which controls this power, and, of course, your right to use this power according to free choice. Now we must look at the mechanism by which you control this power. Here is a new definition. *Magick is the science of using and understanding the power of the subconscious mind.*

No matter what the books, experts, or anyone else may care to say, the real seat of power lies within your subconscious mind. This incredible part of your mind knows no limits other than the ones you give it. It is important that you think about this carefully—no limits other than the ones which you define by belief. In other words, your limits, both magically and in life, are entirely yours. Change those limits, expand them, and you automatically expand your life. Conversely, narrow your limits and you restrict your life.

Remember that your subconscious mind responds to your wishes and beliefs, and if those beliefs are expansive, optimistic, and progressive, then good fortune and happiness flows into your life. By contrast, if the beliefs are narrow and restrictive, then poverty, illness, and lack are bound to materialize. In either case, your subconscious mind responds fully to the wishes (beliefs) which you give it.

Let me illustrate how this is possible when people decide to widen their horizons and defy the apparent facts or norms. Take, for example, Roger Bannister who, many years ago, decided that he could break the barrier of the four minute mile. He believed that he could do this and so he did break the supposed barrier, despite what everyone else thought! Human beings flew faster than sound and eventually walked on the surface of the Moon as a direct result of various people widening their horizons and believing that these things were possible. The list of expanding horizons is almost endless if you choose to look.

Now look at some really impossible feats, such as firewalking, in which human beings walk barefooted over redhot coals without any injury. No, this is not a fake or a clever trick; it actually happens. Do you know how this is done? I have seen men eat broken glass and razor blades, again without injury; needles are pushed into arms and legs without pain; and even a solid steel skewer can be pushed through a man's neck without so much as a drop of blood being spilled. How do people do these things? The answer is quite simple: they use the power of the subconscious mind.

From the opposite point of view, much trouble can easily be brought into a person's life by adopting narrow limits and negative beliefs. More and more, the medical profession is having to admit that the bulk of illnesses are due to psychosomatic causes. In other words, the cause is all in the mind—that is, the subconscious mind. This is one reason why the placebo works. The patient is convinced that this new pill contains a wonder drug and so he or she gets well. Both you and I know that sugar is unlikely to cure anything. It is belief that effects the cure. The horizons have been lifted and the limits have been expanded.

Good and Evil

As far as your subconscious mind is concerned, there is no difference between good and evil. This may sound confusing or even ridiculous but, nevertheless, it happens to be true. If you ask a computer to work out a complex calculation, it will do so without effort. If you ask another computer to fire a nuclear missile at some enemy, it will also carry this out. It is not concerned with morals, judgments, rights, and wrongs; it simply does what you tell it to do without question. The difference between the two computers is only the type of program which has been given to the computer. Those programs were conceived by human beings, not by the computer itself. This wonderful electronic machine acts on instructions. By itself, it can do nothing until these instructions are given. The subconscious mind is exactly comparable. It responds to your instructions but does not, by itself, pass judgment on them. Good and evil, right and wrong, sensible or stupid, kind or unkind, or any other polarization that you can think of, mean nothing to the subconscious. At first glance, this may seem like an absurd way of handling power, but if you look a little deeper you will see the wisdom in it.

Free Choice

This is the answer to the riddle. All the great achievements, and, indeed, all the horrors that the world has ever seen, are entirely due to the way in which people think. That is, they think in such a way as to cause their subconscious mind to actualize those thoughts. Forget about God's will, fate, destiny, or any other of those intangibles which are normally blamed (or praised) for these events. They are all caused by human beings! If this is true, and I assure you that it is true, you must logically come to the conclusion that we all have free choice. More to the point, you have to also accept that the subconscious minds which actuate these thoughts did not know of good and evil. Think about this again and again, because this way of looking at life solves many of life's riddles, and explains why we have such a mixture of miracles and catastrophes.

Cause and Effect

It is quite reasonable to assume that every effect must have a cause. In other words, nothing can ever exist until someone causes it to exist in the first place. We, as human beings, have the distinction of being able to create, or cause things to happen, by using our subconscious minds. Naturally, we are therefore responsible for the effect that each thought has. This responsibility is very real, and much has been made of this by dogmatic fools, and those who wish to have power over others through fear. In truth, there is nothing to fear except fear. Contrary to popular belief, God is not sitting up there taking stock of all your mistakes so that you will not be able to escape paying for your mistakes. This is absurd. In addition, that ludicrous concept named karma is equally absurd and should be rejected in favor of truth.

Cause and effect explains everything. You are bound to be responsible for everything which you create, be it physical or nonphysical. Whether this is done knowingly or unknowingly, you are still responsible. This does not mean that there are debts to pay, and it certainly does not mean that you will have to pay them in some future life.

If you drop a pebble into a pool (cause), it will produce ripples which will eventually reach the edge (effect). So it is with your thoughts and actions; they will affect whatever they come into contact with, whether things or people. Just like ripples which will eventually return back to the center of the pool, so the effect of thoughts is bound to come back to you. This is not divine retribution, it is scientific fact.

The lesson to be learned is simply one of knowing yourself and controlling your thoughts, in order to get better results from the laws of cause and effect.

Influencing the Subconscious

If every fleeting thought influenced the subconscious mind, our lives would be impossible, again due to cause and effect. Fortunately this is not the case. It requires a certain quality of thought to stimulate the subconscious into action. This is a very useful safety mechanism. There are many ways to influence your subconscious. Among the more obvious methods are: prayer, strong desire, affirmations, positive (or negative) thinking, hypnosis, altered states of consciousness, measured gnostic conjuration, meditation, and, of course, outright belief.

There is no need for me to go into detailed description of these techniques. If you wish to explore these subjects, there are many books available. It will suffice to say that these subjects are side-branches of the great science of Magick. With the exception of hypnosis, we will use all of these techniques together with other specialized ideas which belong only to Magick.

Symbols

A symbol is a sign plus an associated concept. The subconscious mind does not understand the English language, or, indeed, any other language which exists on this Earth. It can only understand symbols. Before words can have any effect, they have to be translated into symbols by the mind.

This is not as difficult as you may think. In fact you do it automatically, all the time.

In order to understand this mechanism, try this example yourself. Say to yourself, "I feel good." The net result will be no effect. You have simply spoken a few words. Now try this. Say to yourself, "I FEEL GOOD." Do this many times and try to get involved and absorbed in the idea of FEELING good.

Now, notice the difference. The quality of thinking has changed and more important, you have been putting an imaginary picture in your mind. Your thoughts have been translated into feelings and pictures. Those pictures are symbolic; they are words which have now been translated into a language that the subconscious mind can understand.

Sustained, determined thinking such as this gets results because the quality of thought has been changed, and your subconscious mind recognizes the difference. This is one reason why the words of power published in books can work, but usually do not. Unless these words are spoken with feeling and determination, they will remain ineffective words.

There are many types of symbols. Each has its use in Magick. Without going into complications at this stage, it will suffice to say that without symbols, Magick cannot work. The technique here described is the basis of mind power and, by itself, if used correctly, is bound to get results. However, there are other uses of symbols which enhance this considerably. These involve working within a symbolic framework. There are many names for this. We will use the term, Cosmic Inworld. The construction of this inworld began with the use of the Inner Temple; we will extend this idea and discuss it later on. For now I will simply point out that, like all true magical techniques, it is not a difficult task.

The Universal Mind

It is impossible to overestimate the vast power of the subconscious mind. This remarkable facet of your being is the best servant you could ever wish for, because it will do whatever you ask, once you know how. The subconscious mind is literally the God within, your own Genie, if you like.

Your subconscious is in contact with everything in creation, but not only that; it is also in direct contact with every other subconscious mind in existence. It really is limitless! When you give it an instruction, it automatically carries it out by directing energy on your behalf. However, it also seeks the cooperation of all the other subconscious minds. This makes it quite formidable when activated. Never apply normal human limitations to a subconscious mind. They do not apply! Let me give you an example.

Suppose that you gathered around you about one hundred people selected at random, and then collectively asked them to lend you $1,000. If you were fortunate, you may raise about $5.00, and you certainly would get a lot of strange looks, together with many abusive comments. Quite naturally, human feelings and thoughts would get in the way. Now, if you ask your subconscious mind to get you the same amount, it will get that cooperation from others because human feelings and failings cannot get in the way. They do not exist within your subconscious mind (remember, it does not know about good and evil). Your subconscious will always get the full cooperation of everything and everybody concerned. Like God, it always seeks to supply.

One lesson which should be learned right away is that there really is no need to try to force others into parting with what they have. All you have to do is ask (in the right way), and it is brought into being by your subconscious mind without harming anyone. The way to success and to the acquisition of real power is by using your subconscious mind. This is your right, it is also the way of real Magick.

The Real Magick Circle

1. Read through this chapter over and over again. Think about the ideas presented to you. Consider these carefully. They form the basis of a belief pattern which not only works, but also happens to be true.
2. SECRECY is a vital part of all magical work. In the same way that you can influence your subconscious mind to get results, others may well try to work against you because of jealousy, envy, and so forth. They may do this deliberately or inadvertently; however, the point to remember is that their thoughts also influence their own subconscious minds, and if these thoughts are in opposition to your own, you may find difficulties which get in the way. Keep your magical work to yourself.
3. Finally, we will put together the principles you have learned in this chapter. Find a quiet place and relax. It often helps if you listen to soft music and burn some incense or joss sticks.

The next part is learning to construct the beginnings of a Cosmic Inworld. This is done by bringing in the idea of the magical circle. Forget all the nonsense which has been written about Magick Circles, some of which really is absurd. A true Magick Circle exists in the mind, and is a very potent symbol. To erect this, simply use your imagination in the following way.

Start by imagining a point of light immediately in front of you; then see this point travel in a clockwise direction until it forms a circle of light around you. Practice this many times. It often helps if you use key words such as:

"Cosmos arise." Imagine the point of light and then the circle. At the conclusion of any work say: "Cosmos cease." Reverse the procedure by seeing the circle disappear in a counterclockwise direction.

When you are proficient in this technique, extend it like this: first perform the "quickening of the subconscious exercise" (page 15), and then erect the Magick Circle, and contemplate the following ideas. The Magick Circle contains ALL in existence. ALL is possible within this Magick Circle, and nothing harmful can exist within this Magick Circle. This symbol, being recognized by the subconscious mind, will eventually become a bridge between yourself and power. Practice this often.

The final stage is to erect the circle and then perform the Inner Temple Exercise (see page 35). Follow this through until you reach the pool, and have your desire list at hand. Now, remembering the ideas given to you concerning quality thinking, look at each one and affirm, "I shall have . . . [name desire or need]." Do this several times while being determined and while putting feeling into these words. Look into the pool and into your imagination. See yourself having the very thing you desire. Do not let conscious thoughts, such as, "This is impossible," or, "If only," get in the way. Push these to one side, relax, and indulge yourself in what seems to be a dream or fantasy. Do not rush; take your time. Hopes and wishes never get results. Constructive, creative thinking, such as this, sow seeds into the fertile ground within your subconscious mind. At conclusion leave the Inner Temple by the door and close down the circle.

In Magick and in life, there is no such thing as something for nothing. Input = Output. The more you practice, the quicker the results, so practice often and learn to accept the fact that you really do have the power to transform your life, and that your subconscious mind is there to help in every way possible, if you ask.

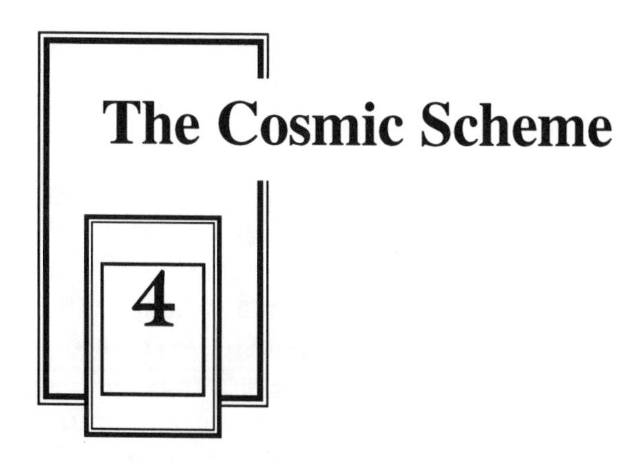

4 The Cosmic Scheme

Magick is the science of using your subconscious mind to gain whatever you wish from life. Any magical theory which does not include this idea is completely wrong. This is one reason why many magical operations simply do not work, or only succeed up to a point. The more ludicrous ideas will not work at all, while some of the others *may* work, if you try hard enough. In truth, you can make anything work, if you believe in it but, quite often, these patterns of belief are completely divorced from truth. This makes discovery of one's own power a long drawn-out process. At best, you may gain some success after years of struggle, at worst, nothing happens. Granted, there are a number of magicians who will grudgingly concede this paradigm, but in order to be a successful contemporary magician, I feel that you should embrace this paradigm! By taking such a plunge, you simultaneously improve your technique, confirm your results, confound your critics, and make an honest person of yourself. Do not worry about betraying some great tradition, Magick has always been motivated by the subconscious mind. Do not worry about being "scientific," the scientists do not know what the subconscious mind is, and most of them will admit that they do not. What is needed is a complete clearance of the mind's rubbish, followed by the establishment of a commonsense basis from which one can discover the truth about Magick.

The Power of the Subconscious

The subconscious mind is the key to all magical practices, so it makes sense to learn as much as you can about it. The first idea to grasp is that the subconscious mind has no limitation whatsoever. It is most important that you keep this fact in your mind. Your subconscious mind has instant connection to everything in creation and everything behind creation simultaneously. Time and space mean nothing, and nothing can ever be impossible or beyond its power. If, by any chance, this description is beginning to sound like God, do not be surprised. We are told that humankind was created in the image of God. We are also informed, "We are gods." These are not idle or romantic statements, they are absolute truth. The kingdom of God does indeed lie within you, it is your own God-center—your subconscious mind. Therefore, you, like God, have the ability to create using the limitless power of your subconscious mind, while still exercising your right of free choice. The subconscious mind's limitless power is largely due to connections. Let me explain.

The Subconscious and Universal Intelligence

Behind all power and manifestation, there is a supreme intelligence which can be described as God. This all-knowing God has the answer to all things, and is quite willing to give you access to this knowledge. In addition, Universal Intelligence seeks only to help you achieve that which you desire. It does not seek to control you in any way, shape, or form, nor does it seek to restrict or withhold. It is totally beneficial. Believe that God is there to help; in doing so you can open the channels of power and knowledge. By believing, you activate your subconscious mind, which has direct connection to God. If you ask of God, you will always receive, because your asking stimulates the subconscious mind which, in turn, passes the request on to God. The idea of a hotline to heaven is really not as farfetched as people may think when you start to consider this idea. You will also notice that there is now no need for a self-styled mediator. Through your subconscious mind, you can contact God direct!

The Subconscious and Universal Energy

Your subconscious mind has the capacity to handle energy and direct this toward whatever objective is selected. Universal Energy is abundant and freely available. There are no restrictions on its use, nor is it ever likely to run out. Everything contains energy, or life force, as it is sometimes described. There are also innumerable types of energy to account for the countless variations in physical phenomena we experience. Your subconscious mind knows every type of energy, and also knows which type to use in any given situation. All that you have to do is select your objective and the subconscious mind does the rest.

The Subconscious and Universal Mind

Everyone has a subconscious mind and all of these minds are connected together. Many paranormal phenomena can be explained by this connection. Clairvoyance, telepathy, and healing are among the obvious ones. Reincarnation or "past lives" are also easily explained through this linkage. For instance, your subconscious mind has a vast memory, it retains everything that you experience. In addition, being linked to the Universal Mind, you also have access to the memories of everyone else, past or present. How easy it is to regress back in time and experience another life! But was this your life, or were you experiencing the life of someone else through the Universal Mind? Remember what has been written concerning the laws of life. There is no compulsion by any force outside yourself, so how can anyone be forced to reincarnate? This is absurd. The universal linkage makes sense; reincarnation may be an unfounded belief, a misconception, or a pseudo-ideal, and so you are advised to abandon it in favor of truth. Remember that your beliefs can work both ways, either they can bring untold success or they can restrict you. Silly dogmas, such as reincarnation and karma, will do nothing other than restrict you. You are advised to throw these out.

The laws of cause and effect are, however, accurate and dependable. Whatever you project, you will get back. This is very important when dealing with the Universal Mind. If, for instance, your inner thoughts and beliefs are negative, aggressive, or off-putting, other people will pick these up on subconscious levels, no matter what you project on the surface. They will then cooperate with these thoughts; in other words, you will receive little help. Note that others are not necessarily seeking to destroy you or harm you in any way, they are simply reacting to these inner thoughts that you are sending out. Fortunately, the reverse is true.

The action of the Universal Mind can easily be seen if you look around. Notice the difference between those people who seem to attract all the good things in life as opposed to those who are selfish and self-opinionated. The latter know only lack.

Symbolism

Getting the subconscious to accept instructions is what Magick is all about, and this is not as difficult as may, at first, be supposed. It does, however, need some practice and study if you are to gain the undoubted benefits that Magick can bestow.

There are two aspects to magical work—the outer and the inner. Let us look at the inner work first. The subconscious responds to three types of stimuli. These are the mind, the emotions, and the imagination. All three must be utilized in any meaningful magical ritual and you will be shown how to do this in a perfectly easy and natural way. It is, however, the imagination that gets results.

Everyone has the capacity to imagine, it is quite natural. Daydreaming is a form of imagination, albeit an unproductive use of this faculty. The use of the imagination should not be confused with visualization techniques prescribed by certain writers. Visualization is simply an exercise in concentration, and while there are certain advantages in training the mind to concentrate, these are best left alone until you really feel the need to explore this avenue. Most writers of mind power books confuse visualization with imagination. There is quite a difference, and the end result is completely different.

First let me illustrate what the imagination is. Without looking, describe a daffodil. Stop and think about this.

Now, I am not so much interested in your actual description as in the way in which you arrived at it. You used your imagination by calling up a picture from memory. Now let us try something a little different. I want you to describe your ideal home. Do not read any further until you have tried this. Take your time and really think about this slowly and deliberately.

By now, you should have a reasonably good idea of your ideal home: what it looks like, where it is, and what furniture and decorations are in it. Again, you used your imagination, except this time you were not only drawing up images from memory, you were creating a picture in your mind. This is part of the secret of using the imagination.

Your subconscious mind responds to images created in the mind, providing that you do this in a certain way. This is important, for if every image was acted on, life would be a hopeless shambles! In order to get the subconscious mind to respond, you have to bring in the mind and the emotions. This is your safety mechanism. Unless you put deliberate thoughts and feelings into these pictures, nothing happens. It is a well-known fact (which you can prove) that if you hold a picture in your mind of what you want while believing that you will receive this, you are bound to get your wish. This is due to the fact that the imaginary picture is being presented to your subconscious mind in the right way by exerting positive thinking and sustained desire.

These imaginary pictures are symbolic. They represent an idea, concept, or ideal. The other type of symbol is one that is purely abstract. It is the use of abstract symbols that makes the difference between mind power and Magick. Let us now examine these in detail to see how we can use them best.

The Encircled Cross

To save lengthy description, see figure 2 (page 57). The Encircled Cross is the master symbol from which all other magical symbols emanate; it also equates to the magician's Magick Circle. Do forget about those strange stories of magicians, standing in their Magick Circles, calling up the devil, or alternatively, fending off hordes of demons and other assorted entities. This is simply ridiculous and those who insist on treating the science of Magick in this way are deluding themselves.

The true Magick Circle exists in your mind, not on the floor of some temple. Its purpose is not to exclude the hordes of hell; it is used to activate the subconscious mind in a rather special way. Let us now look at the correct way in which the Magick Circle should be used in Magick.

Symbols convey a vast amount of information to those who take the trouble to use them properly. It is outside the

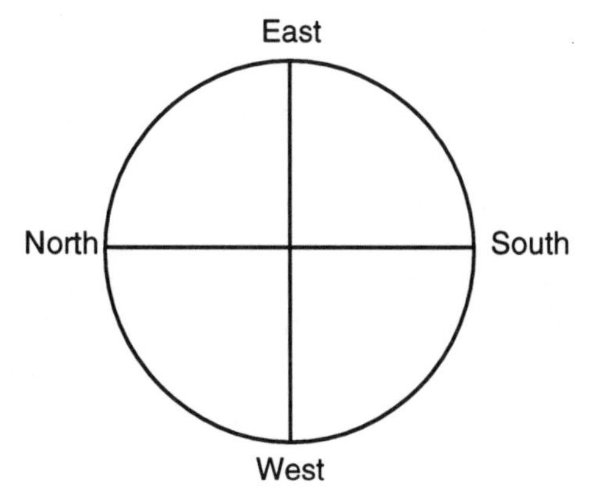

Figure 2. The Encircled Cross.

scope of this present work to go into any great detail on this, for the study of symbols best belongs to Esoteric Magick. However, here is a brief guide to the mysteries of the Encircled Cross.

The central point represents your inner power; in other words, your subconscious mind. The circle represents everything in creation that has existed, or will ever exist; it encompasses all. From center to circumference, there are four arms, or paths. These are the paths along which your subconscious mind directs power to achieve physical results. The four points at which these paths intersect the circle are named the *cardinal points* and each cardinal point is governed by an *element*.

The Four Elements

In case you are not familiar with the elements, I will now give you some idea of how these function. All physical objects consist of two distinct parts, inert matter and life energy. Life energy can be symbolically represented by the four elements. It would be true to say that the difference between two objects, say, granite and lead, lies simply in the nature of the energy which each contains. Both granite and lead are made of inert matter. The energy contained in them is, however, quite different. So what is different about these energies? The answer lies in the makeup of the energy in terms of the elements; in other words, the mixture and balance is different. If you think of how many different types of pastry could be produced from flour, water, shortening, and eggs, you will soon grasp the basic idea. It is not necessary to know every single elemental combination, or even which of these belongs to a certain object. Your subconscious already knows this. All that you need concern yourself with is the fact that your subconscious mind works through the four elements to achieve results. The elements are therefore important from this point of view. Let us now continue by learning how to erect this symbol in the mind.

Stage One

Before any magical act, slow down, relax, and become calm, while pushing aside all everyday thoughts. Perform the quickening of the subconscious exercise (page 15). Peace and power go together. When you have finished the exercise, feel that you are filled with power and energy. Now imagine a point of bright light inside yourself, at about heart level. See this grow and get brighter. Now imagine a beam of light traveling from your heart to some convenient point immediately in front of you. This forms the first arm of the cross which terminates at the cardinal point of east. It should be noted that magical east always lies in front of you. Now imagine a similar beam of light traveling toward your right, at about the same distance.

This ends at magical south. A similar beam is now sent out behind you toward magical west, and finally, the fourth arm is seen to travel out toward your left, ending at magical north. All that remains to be done is to add the circle. Simply imagine that this starts at magical east as a circle of light which travels in a clockwise direction around the magical points, finishing at east once more. The Magick Circle and Encircled Cross are now complete.

This procedure is known as opening the circle. To close down, reverse the procedure, finally seeing the light within your heart disappear. Always remember that all magical work should have some form of opening formula and that, at the end of any magical work, there must be some means of closing down. The two are essential as they act as an on/off switch to your subconscious. Practice this stage often until you are proficient before moving on to the next stage.

Stage Two

The next stage is to convert the flat circle into a three-dimensional Cosmic Sphere. See figure 3 (page 60). Start with the central light within your heart, but before projecting the four arms of the cross, imagine a beam of light traveling upward to a distance equal to the arms of the cross. Similarly, imagine a beam of light traveling downward, again to the same distance. Now erect the circle as before. All that remains to be done is to complete the Cosmic Sphere by adding two more circles. Start at the top and imagine a circle of light traveling to south, base, north, and back to top. The final circle is constructed by starting at the top once more, this time traveling toward east, base, west, and finally back to top again. You now have the triple rings of cosmos which surround a Cosmic Sphere. To close this down, simply reverse the procedure once more.

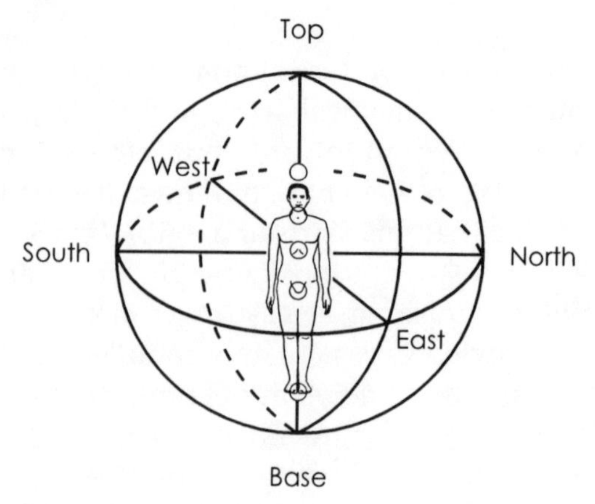

Figure 3. The Cosmic Sphere.

Practice this stage as often as possible. This need not be done in a temple or room set aside for magical work; the exercise can be done anywhere.

The Cosmic Sphere and the Imagination

You may wonder how it is possible to see the Cosmic Sphere in the mind's eye while imagining something else, such as opening the elemental gateways and seeing the pool of water; in other words, imagining two things at once.

It is all a question of memory. To imagine several different things all at the same time would of course be difficult if not impossible. Fortunately you do not need to do this. As you build up the Cosmic Sphere you establish each part in your memory, moving on through each successive stage, concentrating only on whatever is necessary. For instance, you start with the central light, imagining that this exists; then your attention moves on to the next stage of imagining the first of the six arms. There is no need to keep the image of the central light constantly in your imagination because it is presumed to exist, and in fact does exist in your memory. We use this and similar procedures in everyday life. For instance, suppose you were standing in a room facing a window. You would see the window quite clearly. Now if you turned around to face the opposite wall, you would, of course, see the wall instead. However, you would still know that the window existed, because you had just seen this. In fact, you could recall this in your imagination because its image is stored in your memory. In a similar fashion, having become familiar with the room, you would know what the room looked like in totality without actually seeing this physically.

It is exactly the same with the Cosmic Sphere and inner SEEING; in other words, using your imagination to build up an imaginary room in your memory. All through the building-up procedure, you establish each stage before moving on to the next. Therefore, at the pool you are free to concentrate on this, knowing that the Cosmic Sphere and Inner Temple exist in your memory because you have put them there.

At the end of the ritual it is necessary to inform your subconscious mind that these are no longer established, hence the need for a closing procedure. Never forget that although this Cosmic Sphere and Inner Temple are imaginary, it would be easy to dismiss the entire concept as being worthless, this is not the case. Any deliberate erection of a symbolic pattern will have an effect on the subconscious mind, because you are using what is, in effect, a powerful language which the subconscious understands. It is, therefore, necessary to treat these symbols with respect, and practice using them often.

Magical Rituals

At this point in the book, we should examine what a ritual is and how it works. Before any ritual can work, it has to be constructed according to sensible principles and it must have a large degree of personal involvement. Far better that you construct your own rituals to suit your needs. This book will help you do this. Let us now look at the components of magical ritual.

A magical ritual is a means of concentrating the mind by bringing together those things which are sympathetic to the nature of the energy being used. Naturally, the intention of the ritual will dictate which energy, and consequently which ritual equipment, will be needed. Guidance will be given throughout this book as to the best choice of energy and ritual equipment. The correct procedure for performing a ritual is as follows:

1. Think carefully about the intention.
2. Plan the ritual.
3. Prepare for the ritual.
4. Perform the ritual or series of rituals.
5. Back up the ritual with creative thinking.

The Intention

This should be considered carefully from all angles, bearing in mind what has already been written. It is vital that you think positively about your intention. There is simply no use performing a ritual if your mind is filled with doubts and uncertainties. Know what you want, and be *determined* that you are going to get it! By far the greatest cause of failure is trying to perform a rite while hoping and wishing that some god or external entity may (if it so chooses) grant your request. Do not subscribe to this sort of thinking. Remember, the way in which you ask determines what you get. So if you stand there, knees trembling, and heart thumping, flinging cries of desperation toward the heavens, *nothing will happen!* Know what you want, then believe that you are about to have this.

Planning a Ritual

Having decided on your intention, you must now plan the rite. Careful consideration should be given to the choice of magical equipment to be used. The golden rule: the intention dictates the type of energy to be used, so this energy will, in turn, dictate the type of ritual equipment to be used. For example, if you were performing a healing ritual, the energy used would be that which equates to the Sun, therefore all equipment, robes, incense, and so forth should be chosen accordingly. Specific ritual items will be discussed later on when we deal with the planets but, for now, keep the basic idea in mind. It should always be understood that magical equipment is not, in itself, magical. The Magick lies within YOU, in your ability to influence your subconscious mind. The true purpose of magical equipment is solely to act as a focus for the mind. This may be done in several ways.

Color: Different colors suggest different ideas. For instance, red suggests energy, while green suggests peace. You would not consider using black robes, candles, or altar cloths for a healing rite, would you? No, it is the wrong color. Choosing the right color has, up to now, been the subject of much speculation and a great deal of confusion. You will be taught the correct colors, based on reality.

Scent: As with color, scents suggest ideas. Good quality ritual incense is a real asset to any magician. Do not buy cheap incense from magical supermarkets that lay claim to ancient documents or whatever. If you want good incense, buy this from a reputable incense blender.

Shape: This is the third type of ritual aid. Generally, the shape is used symbolically to represent the intention (i.e., an image doll, graphic sigil) or the type of energy being used (an altar symbol). Again, examples will be given at the appropriate time.

Ritual Preparations

There is much to be gained in planning a ritual. First, it eliminates the chances of ruining the ritual because some item has been forgotten; and second, it helps you get involved in what you are doing. Halfhearted efforts reap their own rewards. With Magick, input = output. The more time you spend in planning, the better the results. Do not forget to attend to everyday matters, such as taking the phone off the hook, locking the door, and so forth.

Preliminaries attended to, all that remains is to perform the ritual. Always adopt the sensible approach of relaxing and clearing the mind before you start. When you are calm, cast your mind over the intention while being positive about this. If you have any doubts, fears, or uncertainties, now is the time to remove these. When this has been done, all that remains is to perform your ritual using the guidelines which you will be given. At the conclusion, put everything away and return to normal. It is a good idea to have a magical notebook in which you can list the rites performed, plus the time and date, and any impressions you may have. These notes, which should be brief, will often prove useful later.

Creative Thinking

If your ritual has been performed with anything like conviction and determination, your subconscious mind will now start to bring your desire to fruition. There are, however, some problems which bear thinking about.

No matter what you may have heard or read to the contrary, a single ritual is no guarantee of success, especially in the early stages. Lack of experience is the main problem, and there are several ways to get round this. You can perform the same ritual over a period, or you can use creative thinking. In any case, often the problem is not one of getting your subconscious to respond, it is rather one of keeping the channels open. There is always the chance that negative thinking, such as worry, concern, doubts, and fears, may well get in the way. Note that, providing the ritual has been performed correctly, these things cannot prevent success. They can, however, slow things down. To prevent this happening and to back up any ritual, I would suggest that you spend some time, each day, in creative thinking exercises. These are described shortly.

As your experience grows and your technique improves, you will find that the one-shot ritual does indeed work. This, after all, is the whole point of the exercise. It does need patience and practice to become proficient, so take your time.

Once a method has been found that will produce the desired effect, then it is possible to follow one ritual with another. The ability to clear the subconscious mind of one train of thought and replace it with another is the essential ingredient for follow-on rituals. It is obviously inconvenient to take a bath between intentions, and this is where silent meditation proves invaluable. After the first intent is dealt with, sit quietly for a few moments. Imagine a light like water washing over your entire being; a physical action can accompany this, a ritual washing of hands in a small bowl of scented water is a technique used by many magicians.

Another equally useful method is to extinguish all candles and so forth from the first rite. Sit quietly in the darkness for a few moments and then relight new candles, appropriately colored for the second rite. It is also better to use a general incense on these occasions such as temple, ritual, or meditation. Again, any technique which helps you clear the mind of one intention and make it receptive to another is useful and should be used. Trial and error are always the best way. What will work for one person will not necessarily work for another. Experiment and find your own way, that is your only true path.

Activating the Power of the Cosmic Sphere

Here now is a full-scale ritual based on the principles given in this chapter. Before you attempt this, read through this chapter many times and think deeply about the ideas therein.

Start by selecting your intention. Choose this with care and, above all else, make it realistic. Most people make the mistake of aiming too high. It is far better to start small, gradually building on each success and learning as you go. It is, at this stage, all a question of belief and this should become your guiding light. For example, if lack of money is a problem, it is generally quite pointless to perform a ritual to win some giant lottery. In any case, if everyone did this, there would not be enough left to be worth sharing out! The main problem would be one of belief. In other words, would you really be confident, at this stage, that you would win, or would you be hoping? There is quite a difference. It is far easier to conceive the acquiring of, say, $100 than it is to acquire $1,000,000. If you really want to be a millionaire then, by all means, keep this in mind. This should, in any case, be on your desire list for future reference. It is always more realistic to start small when dealing with rituals, gradually working down the list as you become more confident.

Having sorted out your ritual intention, plan your ritual using the principles already given. The only pieces of magical equipment you will need are a candle, a suitable holder, and something that will act as an altar. The latter can be a dressing table, small cupboard or whatever comes to mind. Clear it of any existing items and cover it with a clean cloth. An incense burner or joss stick holder may also be placed on the altar.

Relax and clear the mind, then think about your intention carefully and deliberately, building up positive thoughts. When ready, light the candle, which is a symbolic representation of your inner power. Pause and consider this. Any incense or joss sticks may now be lit. The next stage is to erect the Cosmic Sphere as described earlier. Then enter the Inner Temple, right up to the point of looking into the central pool; this, of course, may be done as a seated meditation.

Having opened the Cosmic Sphere and entered the Inner Temple, you now come to the main part of the ritual—giving your subconscious mind instructions. There are many ways to do this. All will be discussed in later chapters, but for now, here is a suggestion. All you have to do is imagine that, right in front of you, is the now familiar pool in the Inner Temple. This is symbolic, and represents your subconscious mind. The actual water represents Universal Energy. Do not be put off by the simplicity of this: your subconscious will understand what you are doing because you are giving it symbols which it fully comprehends. Move toward the pool, and with your finger, write the intention on the surface of the water. This need not be a long-winded description. Use the minimum number of words such as "extra money," "better health," and so forth. Now, see the pool change to a fountain which rises high into the air and glows with bright light. Spend as long as you like with this image in your imagination. At the conclusion, see the fountain revert back to a calm pool once more; then leave the Inner Temple and close down the Cosmic Sphere. If you are using a bedroom or other temporary temple, clear everything away.

I would suggest that you now back up the ritual with a creative thinking exercise. This should be performed at least once a day for about ten or fifteen minutes. To do this, sit down, relax, and clear the mind, then erect the Cosmic Sphere. Now, spend some time thinking about your intention in a positive way. By far the best method is to imagine that you actually have the thing you desire. This may seem like daydreaming or a waste of time. Let me assure you that it is not! The actual mechanism is quite complex, so it will suffice to say that by doing this you are keeping the channels of power open in a safe and natural way. See your desire coming toward you, see yourself having it, be optimistic and expect it to find its way to you. It will if you provide the channel.

You can also use these creative thinking sessions to think about all the other desires on your list, as this helps you keep them in mind, in addition to preparing the way for subsequent magical rituals.

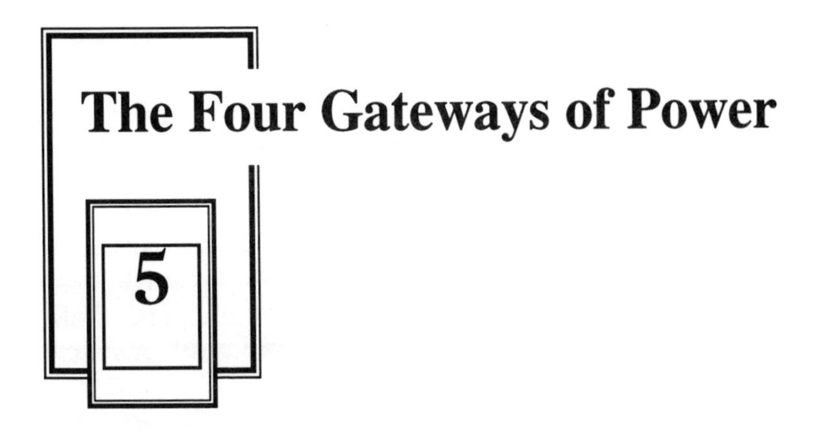

5 The Four Gateways of Power

If you desire success in your magical work, there are two approaches to be considered. These are 1) acquisition of power, and 2) removal of obstacles. Always consider magical work to be rather like a coin: there are two sides; each one different, yet both are an integral part of the whole.

Always look on the bright side. Here, we are dealing with the acquisition of power and potential. Nothing less will do. True magical success depends on sound basic technique and positive thinking at all times.

The techniques given in this book are totally reliable. Use them, think about them, and build on them in your own way and you will not go far wrong. There are no shortcuts to success, you must work for it. Remember the law—input = output.

Likewise, do nothing unless you fully understand what you are doing. If you fail to observe this rule, you are bound to lose because, apart from being uncertain within yourself, you are giving confusing instructions to your subconscious mind. Naturally the results are bound to be disappointing.

The truest words ever spoken are, "Thoughts create things." You are constantly creating around yourself all kinds of things in direct proportion to the quality of your dominant thoughts. It naturally follows that the more positive your thoughts are, especially from a magical point of view, the better the results in a physical sense. Once again, the input = output law proves itself, for *as you think, so you are.* This can work for or against you, so it becomes essential to cultivate belief.

Time and time again you will read or hear that you must believe. A wise man once said, "If thou canst believe, all things are possible to him that believeth" (Mark 9:23). Not "some things." There is no implication of "if," "except," or "perhaps." All things are implied and meant! Now do not try to give me the excuse that you cannot believe as such. You believe that the sky is blue or that 2 + 2 = 4. You believe these to be true yet there is no factual evidence to support them. Let me explain.

Where did you acquire the knowledge that the sky is blue? From someone else. Where did they acquire this knowledge? From someone else. You can repeat this as often as you like until you backtrack to the originator of the definition, who must have, out of necessity, described the sky as blue. What evidence did this person have that it was in fact blue? The answer is none. This person believed it to be blue and so did everyone who followed. Exactly the same can be said of 2 + 2; there is no proof that this does indeed add up to 4, nevertheless we believe it to be true. This is not simply an interesting exercise, it reveals a profound truth to those who are willing to think a little deeper than the obvious. It reveals that our beliefs are not necessarily true, yet all beliefs equate to physical facts. This gives rise to the syndrome, "Which came first, the chicken or the egg?" Are beliefs based on fact, or are facts shaped by beliefs? The former can be true while the latter most certainly is true.

Of vital importance is what you believe, for this is the heart of magical work. Either you accept the beliefs of others, risking self-restriction and possibly inaccurate concepts, or you exercise your right to free choice in what your beliefs are to be. There is always a choice, but only one is correct.

Accept. Just as you accept 2 + 2 = 4. Accept that life will give you whatever you desire providing that you believe or accept that this is, in fact, possible. This is not difficult; after all you can easily accept what, say, the newspapers or the television tell you (even though they are largely wrong) or perhaps believe what "so and so" said (which may again be wrong) without a second thought. So why not accept that life wishes to give you all that you desire? Surely this is a far better pattern of belief than the "norm" created by society? Believe and you shall have. That is the law, the truth, and the way to success in life and in Magick.

Faith is a powerful tool in the right hands because faith is established belief. However, let us get rid of the popular misconceptions concerning faith which have been forced on us. Belief is a tool that can be used to attain desires; faith is acquired when belief is applied totally with persistence until it becomes a habit. Faith, like belief, never fails to get results, because the pattern of belief is now firmly built into the subconscious mind. Have faith in life and its ability to give, and believe that you will have your heart's desire. This is supreme sense, and a major key in Pragmatic Magick, so, like belief, throw out misguided concepts and replace these with truth.

Optimism is a quality severely lacking in today's world. Dogmatism has led humanity to believe that all is lost, or that fate or karma must take precedence over free will. How can anyone be optimistic if he or she believes that life is a foregone conclusion, and that no one has a say in their existence? Thankfully, we do have control, and once this is realized, freedom is the prize. To cultivate optimism is to realize that you do have a choice, and it gives your subconscious mind that extra push, for nothing works miracles quicker than a healthy frame of mind. Imagine the difference between a ritual done in fear, uncertainty, and with a dash of hope, and one performed in confidence and optimism. There can be no doubt as to which ritual procedure succeeds.

To be optimistic is to expect results and success, and if you have digested and understood what has gone before, you will see that optimism is the right attitude of mind to adopt. As you think so you are, is the law, so by being optimistic and expectant, you are opening the paths to the power in the right way. Conversely, being fearful means that you are defeating your own ends before you even start. So do not subscribe to fear. Being optimistic is not really difficult once you get into the habit, for it must be a habit in magical work. Think about all that has been written, think about the vast potential available to you, think of the freedom of choice that you really do have. Be positive in every sense of the word, keep an open mind, and refuse to be dragged down by the ramblings of those who subscribe to self-defeat. Do this and you will achieve optimism, a new habit which will repay you many times over.

Perhaps the greatest cause of ritual failure is that of lack of persistence. This stems from two basic problems which are:

1. The presumption that, especially in the early stages, one ritual will be adequate. When you are adept—in other words, highly skilled—in ritual techniques, and have total belief in what you are doing, one ritual is all that you need. This, however, may take years of practice and study. By far the best approach is to use either a series of rituals over a given period of time or a single, well-planned ritual backed up by regular creative thinking sessions which ensure that the subconscious is kept on target.

2. Giving up before results become apparent, or because negative thinking has been allowed to take precedence over the determination to succeed. It is very easy to give yourself all manner of excuses for failing to persist and reasons not to continue. All too often there is not time or

something has to be done in preference to magical work. Old habits die hard, but die they must, if you are to succeed. Make time and persist; break these bad habits once and for all, and defy negative thinking by taking control of your thoughts, especially the ones which incline you to give up or put things off until some convenient time which inevitably never arrives.

Persistence wins every time because sustained thought cannot fail. The only failure is in not sustaining your original belief or intention. This was the original idea of self-discipline. This has degenerated into all manner of negative ideas such as that of sackcloth and ashes, needless penances, and in some cases, self-flagellation. Self-discipline simply means taking control over body and mind, not by starvation or self-inflicted restrictions, but by shedding bad habits and persisting along a course of action despite all the excuses that the mind can offer.

The opposite side of the coin is concerned with problems that arise from beliefs that stand in the way of progress and attainment. Some have already been discussed, others lie deep within your mind and are largely unrecognized in normal circumstances. It would be impossible to list these in any detail, for they are many and varied; however, they are always a problem to every serious student of Magick. Unlike new beliefs which are accepted out of necessity, these are beliefs of a different fashion in that they are unfounded and self-restricting. Naturally because they are unfounded and therefore untrue, they cause problems which are not easy to spot. In the past, these blocks to power were given various names to aid identification. The old idea of a demon is one of them. In actual fact there is no such thing as a demon. Demons, together with angels, spirits, and similar entities were simply invented to epitomize aspects of human failings or aspirations. These visions of spirits and demons appearing in the

Triangle of Art are actually archetypes evoked from the subconscious mind by the way of Magick Trance. Unfortunately, some people still believe that these things actually exist, which of course is nonsense. The technique of taking some aspect or component of human personality, or cosmos, and creating a sort of personal image, is known as the technique of telesmatics. Unless you fully understand the implications and the problems associated with this, it is best left alone or grave error can result.

Instead of using techniques of the dark ages, it is far better to realize that within each of us there are all manner of negative beliefs which can and do cause problems. It is simply not useful to blame intangibles such as God and the devil, evil spirits, fate, karma, or even bad luck. What we have to do is face the fact that if we fail, it is our own fault whether through bad techniques, lack of belief, or possibly deep-rooted, restrictive beliefs. Blocks to completion are due to the magician or the recipient. Remember that a ritual for healing, say, will not work if the person to be healed does not truly desire this. Matter you can manipulate, as it will always respond to correct magical action. Humans have a will of their own. Blocks may take a long time to discover; it is all a question of effort. The more you look for these the quicker you will be rid of them.

The remedy is usually one of asking: why? If you question with sincerity you will always get answers, because you are asking the source of infinite knowledge within yourself, your subconscious mind. It will always answer if you ask. All you have to do is sit down and take stock of the situation. Try to see where you may have gone wrong, examine the technique you have used, and then examine yourself. Erect your Cosmic Sphere in your mind and ask for an answer; then become calm and expectant. An answer will come, perhaps not immediately, but at some later time and place. When it does come you will know that you have found the answer, and you will also know what to do about the problem. Be prepared for some surprises, however, for as you have asked for the truth, you are likely to learn certain things about yourself that you never suspected. When you do know, act. If you do, the problem is beaten and gone forever, leaving a channel of power open where previously it had been closed. As a final thought, those silly people who practice devil worship and so-called Black Magick can now be seen in a new light, for as there is no devil, these absurd practices can be seen for what they really are. All those people are doing is invoking their very own self-restrictions and deep-rooted fears. This is silly.

Extending the Cosmic Sphere

I hope that by now the Cosmic Sphere has been worked with until it can be easily erected in your mind. If not, spend some time practicing it until it becomes second nature, as this is a vital part of your magical progress, and a foundation for good technique.

Our next task must be one of enhancing the power of this Cosmic Sphere by careful study and application of that which has been learned. You will notice that there are four cardinal points: east, south, west, and north, which together with top and base make up the six nodal points of the Cosmic Sphere. Each point represents a means of contacting and using power, so we will look at these in some detail. See figure 4 (page 76).

Top

This point represents God-power or the All-Father. All religions and patterns of belief imply that God is to be found "up there." In fact, it is now difficult to think of heaven as being anywhere else except above us. Looking upward toward God and the infinite is not some silly superstition; it is a fact as borne out by the geometry of the Cosmic Sphere.

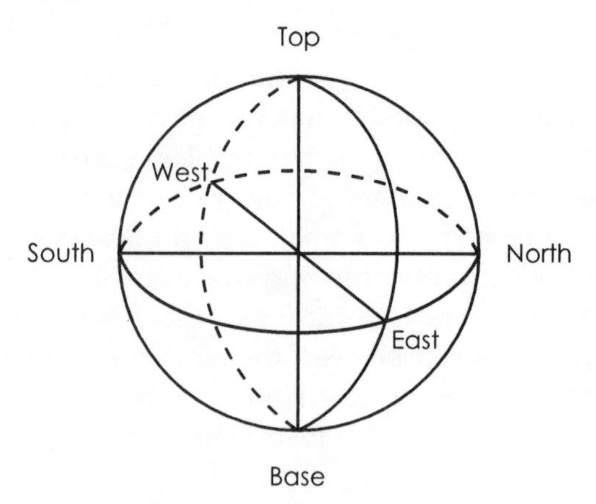

Figure 4. The six nodal points of power.

The fact that God, or Universal Life Energy, is placed above us should not be taken as a sign that, as we are below, we are subservient. This is wrong and unjustified. We, or to be more correct, the essential I, move freely within the Cosmic Sphere, contacting each point for the sole purpose of using the energy and knowledge available. We are not subservient to any point or beneath it in any way. Do forget religious attitudes which tend to creep into Magick from time to time. God, or the God-point above, is directly approachable at all times.

Base

At the base point we contact the *Anima Mundi*, the World-Soul-Earth-Goddess or Earth-Mother and the natural abundance of the Earth epitomized by Nature itself. Nature is prolific and abundant in every sense of the word; there is no lack, neither is there shortage. Take, for instance, any plant. Its sole function appears to be continuation of its species, yet rather than do this according to our plan, it produces numerous flowers which give rise to even more numerous seeds in order to guarantee success. All through Nature you will see this fact, as the overplus is constantly used to startling effect.

The lesson of Nature is simply proliferation, not, as you would think, in a wasteful sense, for Nature also conserves, but rather because abundance is the natural order of things. We, as humans, have forgotten about natural abundance, preferring the strange concept of conservation through fear of shortage. As you now know, whatever we fear (believe) inevitably comes true. Far better to look at Nature and realize that we cannot exhaust the enormous reserves of power which life provides to shape matter according to our needs. The word *Nature* implies all that is natural, and by being natural, in other words accepting the truth about life, we, like Nature, shall indeed become prolific and abundant in every sense.

Whereas the upper point represents pure, directable power, the lower point equates to inert matter being shaped according to our needs, the end product. All-Father gives power, Earth-Mother receives this power and gives it form. The instrument of this transition is, of course, the central point: the subconscious mind. Through this we contact both God and Nature, and by its use we achieve the physical results that we desire. Each point gives in a different fashion, and it should be noted that this giving is total and without restriction.

East

At this first point on the circumference, we come into contact with the four elements of the wise. By far the easiest way to understand these elements is to consider them to be four distinct ways of applying power from above to Earth life. Each element is a mode of action, or a gateway through which a specific type of energy flows. With the eastern point, we meet the element Air. Do not confuse this with its physical equivalent, for although it is similar in nature, it is far more complex and all-embracing.

The eastern point brings us into contact with the conscious mind and our ability to project ourselves by communication on all levels. In particular, it is the realm of the Universal Mind that links us all through past and present into the future. It contains the entire history of the human race and probably the destiny of humankind as well. I hold that its sensitivities extend throughout the solar system and I suspect that it is intrinsically linked to the DNA code. These ideas are philosophically monistic in accordance with the teachings of Hermes Trismegistus and the doctrine of the Cabbala. From a practical point of view, if you wish to learn real magical secrets, then look to the eastern point and the element Air.

South

This is the point at which we meet the element Fire. In a manner similar to physical fire bringing light and heat, the element Fire bestows energy and light. It is the point at which we contact creative impulses, our inner drive and ambitions, and the power to achieve through action and initiative. When you are run-down, you become ill and depleted; you lack fire because your energy levels are low. Little wonder that this element is associated with natural healing or restoration of energy. Acts of courage, daring, and enterprise all belong to Fire, as does illumination in a magical sense.

West

The first two elements are active and positive. With west and north we are dealing with passive and negative elements. It should be noted that the word *negative* is not meant in a derogatory sense. Here, negative means receptive. Likewise, passive does not mean apathetic, it means quietly accepting reality. The western point equates to the element Water. Two things spring to mind, that of fluidity and reflection. Without water, life would be impossible, as most things contain a large percentage of this element. Water flows freely and adapts to whatever shape is willing to accept it, and like the emotions, which are ruled by this element, it can be calm or turbulent. With Water, we are also dealing with the imagination and with the principle of love in its highest form, for just as water sustains life, so Universal Water, or Universal Love, sustain ALL.

North

Our final point is ruled by the element Earth. We began with positive, formless, and almost weightless Air, gradually increasing in density until we now arrive at total solidity and receptivity. Earth is the substance we symbolically mold to our needs, and naturally it plays a vital part in the scheme of things. Without something to shape and receive energy, creation, as such, would not be possible except on purely imaginary levels. Those fools who deny the material side of life, do so at their own peril. They deny their very existence and succumb to the highest of follies, that of failing to recognize the importance of Earth. From a practical point of view, Earth equates to our plan of action, rather than the finished product, for the latter best belongs to the base.

In the four elements we have a perfect plan: think, act, imagine, and plan. All four are necessary if we are to succeed in our aims. Take, for example, the magical process of obtaining a new home. First we would think positively about the intention (Air); we would then become inspired and desire this original idea (Fire); we would work on this in the imagination (Water); within a ritual plan (Earth).

Naturally we would be using power (Top) to achieve the end product (Base).

The Gateways of Power

By far the best way to use the cardinal points is to imagine these as four doorways, or gateways, through which power from above can flow into the Cosmic Sphere to be directed by our subconscious in accordance with our needs. This then flows out through the same gateways to find its fruition at the base. This symbolic scheme can easily be ritualized without expensive equipment or long-winded chants or word-spells. First erect the Cosmic Sphere as usual, following the guidance already given, enter the Inner Temple, and then direct your attention to the upper point. Remember that you are dealing with God-power, or Universal Energy and Universal Intelligence, whose sole purpose is to help in every possible way. Reject all ideas of subservience and unworthiness. They have no basis in fact.

You are dealing with God direct. You are entitled to do this regardless of what dogma dictates. It is your right, so exercise it. Open your mind to Universal Energy and it will oblige. It is this sort of thinking which will set you apart from the many pseudo-magicians and failures who litter the path of real Magick. Putting it bluntly, give God a chance! Forget about normally accepted ideas and open up to this enormous power. You will never regret it.

Now direct attention to the lower point, realizing that you can achieve your desires, and that Nature will respond to your needs and direction, for that is its function. Just as a mother gives, so will Earth yield its abundance at your request. Nothing will ever be denied those who dare to ask of Universal Power and then direct that power into Earth life.

Finally, we make use of the elemental gateways by simply imagining that these exist at the appropriate cardinal points. Look toward the east: see a doorway, and floating in front of it is a Sword. The doorway then opens at your command, revealing the yellow energy of Air. Do this with the other three points using red energy and the Spear at the southern doorway, blue energy and the Chalice at the western doorway, and green energy and the Shield at the northern doorway. Now imagine that power is being generated above, and that this is flowing down toward you. See this pour through the eastern gate as yellow light which plays on the surface of the central pool. Do this with the other three gates using red light at the south, blue light at the west, and green light at the north. Think your intention into the pool, or, as suggested, write this on the surface of the water; then see this pool change into a fountain of light which pours out through the elemental gates, finally impacting on everyday life at the base. Spend some time thinking creatively about this, then close down by seeing the pool become calm, and by closing each door in turn. Complete the ritual by leaving the Inner Temple and closing down the Cosmic Sphere as described in previous chapters.

Magical Equipment

It is very easy for students to waste money on magical equipment. Always remember and apply the golden rules:

1. No equipment is in itself magical. The Magick lies in the way in which you use the equipment. The only exceptions to this rule are those items which have been ritually enhanced for a specific purpose. Magical seals, sigils, and pentacles belong to this group.
2. Each piece of equipment must be symbolic. In other words, it should represent an idea. Never use a ritual item as a focus of worship, or for any other unscientific reason. This is self-defeating and pointless.

Although there are masses of ritual items on sale, you will find most of these to be unnecessary. Items such as Magick Swords, robes, and certain altar symbols do have a place in Magick, but are used to best effect when dealing with esoteric matters where the accent is on ceremonial. As far as this book goes, you will find the following items useful.

Candles. You should have a white central candle, plus a candle for each elemental gateway. The elemental candles can be placed on stands at the correct quarter. They may all be white, but it is better if you use white for center, yellow for east, red for south, blue for west, and green for north.

Altar Symbols. Ideally there ought to be something to represent the four elements. These can be placed on the altar or on the appropriate quarter.

Sword. For the east, the master symbol is the Sword. A small dagger or the Ace of Swords from the tarot deck is useful.

Incense. In the south belongs the incense burner and also the Ace of Wands.

Goblet. For the west, a goblet filled with water is ideal, especially if the water can be obtained from a special place, such as a holy well. Also the Ace of Cups belongs here.

Bowl. For the north, a bowl of earth, again from a magical site if possible. The Ace of Pentacles goes here.

When using the elemental candles, or quarter candles as they are sometimes known, you may light them during the opening of the four gateways to symbolize the fact that power is now flowing into the Cosmic Sphere and Inner Temple.

Working with your Desires

Read through this chapter many times and think carefully about all the ideas given to you. Do not skip over any point, and resist the temptation to rush ahead. Magical work, to be effective, takes patience and practice.

Carefully practice the additional material concerned with extending the Cosmic Sphere and Inner Temple before you start to put it into practice. When you are confident that you can work comfortably with the Cosmic Sphere and Inner Temple then, and only then, should you start to work with your desires. Many magical failures are due to rushing ahead without adequate preparation or without fully understanding the techniques being used.

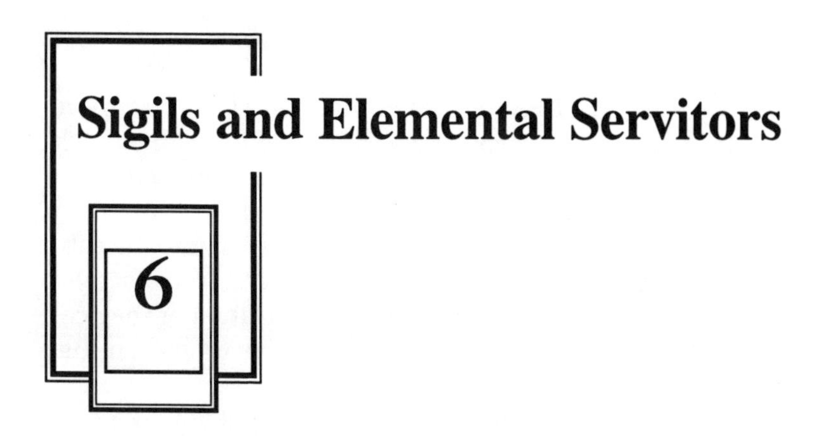

6 Sigils and Elemental Servitors

Sigils act as keys that unlock the power of the subconscious mind. They are personal symbols that act as a language, and the science of Magick makes use of these because they are immediately understood.

Creating Sigils

Sigils are created by combining, stylizing, and fusing the letters of the alphabet together to form an instruction contained in a personal symbol from a sentence of desire. First the desire or intention is written down in capitals: I WISH ACQUISITION OF MY TRUE MAGICAL POWER, after which all repeating letters are omitted. The remaining letters are then condensed into an easily visualizable glyph or sigil. Here is an example:

I WISH ACQUISITION OF MY TRUE MAGICAL POWER.

The following letters now remain from the original formula: H,Q,N,F,Y,G,L,P. You can now design the sigil from these remaining letters. See the finished sigil in figure 5 (page 86). The sigil can also be decorated. Note the little feet placed on the end of each of the three legs. They serve to give the sigil a mystical appearance. It will no doubt take you a few attempts in the beginning to design your sigil; in

Figure 5. The completed sigil.

the latter stages when you have had more practice, you will be able to do this much faster. When you have completed your sigil it will be ready for activation. In other words, you will place it into the subconscious mind. At the end of the activation, using some kind of ritual or magical context, the sigil is destroyed. When this is done, the sigil should be forgotten.

Sigils can be constructed on any material you like. It is traditional to draw these sorts of things on parchment, but nowadays this is not necessary as any good quality paper will do. The only reason parchment became popular was that in olden days it was the only thing available, as paper had not yet been invented, so bear this in mind. Parchment paper is quite a good compromise.

It may well be a good idea to use the same opening command, such as: "MY WISH . . . ," or, "I DESIRE . . . ." The subconscious mind does appear to recognize a regularly used command phrase in time. Your commands should always be formulated clearly; they should not be vague or ambiguous. The idea is to obtain a simple form which can easily be visualized at will.

Flexing Your Psychic Muscles

Before starting these exercises you will find it invaluable to make up a chain of beads—about forty. These can usually be purchased from any art or craft shop. If you have a problem obtaining beads, then use knots instead. The idea behind the use of this chain of beads is that it serves to show how many disturbances happened during your exercise period. Every time you experience an intruding thought or lose an image, just move one bead. By doing this you will know how many interruptions there were.

Nonthinking

Nonthinking is the ability to produce an absolute vacancy of mind. Sit or lie down in a comfortable position, on a bed or couch. Close your eyes and try to stop thinking; nothing is allowed to happen in your mind. Now stay in this state of mind. In the beginning you will only manage this for a few seconds but, with regular practice, the period of time will increase. The purpose of the exercise is completed when you can remain in a nonthinking state for about two minutes. The exercise time may be extended up to five minutes.

Visualization

You will need to develop the ability to hold a clear image or picture in the mind's eye. Put some objects in front of you and relax. The objects may be something like a bottle, a cup, a piece of jewelry, or an ornament. Now fix your eyes on one object and try to remember everything about it—the color and shape. Then close your eyes and try to imagine the object. If it disappears, try to recall it. In the beginning you will only be able to do this for a few seconds. As time goes by, with regular practice, the length of time you can hold the image will actually increase. Practice until you can hold on to it for as long as you like. Use the chain of beads to help keep count of the number of interruptions each time the object or image disappears. Once again, the purpose of the exercise will be completed when you can hold an object or image in your mind's eye without any interruption for about two minutes, without it fading. When this has been achieved, the exercise should be practiced with the eyes open. When this can be done, then the purpose of this exercise is complete. This exercise time may also be extended up to five minutes.

You can also practice using abstract symbols, like planetary glyphs, or the elemental symbols. For example—the circle, triangle, Crescent Moon, or square would all be good images to visualize.

The Magical Trance

This involves using ritual to induce an altered state of consciousness and is much easier to achieve after a period of time known as ritual conditioning. This means you should perform the Cosmic Sphere and Inner Temple exercise, and work with the four elemental gateways for at least twenty-eight days prior to commencing sigil Magick or any other form of ritual Magick. The sigil itself is then concentrated on at the pool, not the desire behind the sigil.

Casting Sigils

In order to cast sigils, the Cosmic Sphere and Inner Temple should be opened up as normal (see pages 35 and 59), right up to the point of changing the pool into the fountain (see page 67). At this point, impress the sigil on the surface of the pool and then conjure the planetary power[1] using the appropriate wording. See the fountain rise high into the air, glowing with energy. Now spend some time holding the sigil in your mind's eye at the peak of the magical trance experience. This is when momentary suspensions of the conscious mind occur, allowing access to subconscious levels. After this, direct the power out of the gateways as before.[2]

[1]A complete discussion of the planetary energies and how you can apply these to solve most of life's problems will be given in Part 2, The Cosmonomicon.
[2]The magician must decide when the sigil has been imprinted on his or her subconscious mind.

The sigil is then symbolically destroyed, perhaps by burning it in the central candle flame, or, if you are using a candle to symbolize the planetary energy, then use this. For the sigil to be successful, it must be forgotten. This is perhaps the hardest part, but it is the key to achieving results.

Concentrating Power into a Ritual

A fully skilled magician should be capable of putting him- or herself into a trance state and maintaining it. It is this ability, which can be acquired only through regular training and practice, that enables the magician to carry out the ritual maneuvers required to concentrate power in a formal operation and still be able to hold the trance. When you can concentrate power correctly, then only a split second is needed. The reason for a lengthy ritual is not to concentrate power for the entire time, unless there are a number of people taking turns and it is virtually impossible for a single person to concentrate pure power for more than a few seconds. Ritual is used to build up power, to gradually raise the level until the moment of release. Start at the mundane level and steadily climb. Each level is emphasized by an action: the lighting of a candle, the burning of incense, an anointing, a conjuration, and so forth. The length of this generating stage depends on each individual; for some it is rapid, for others it is slower, or there may be several high points in which power is released and then the buildup begins again until the next point is reached and so on.

The biggest problem for the beginner is how to know when the time is right, and this is wholly a case of being aware of your magician self and controlling the power patterns of your mind. If you are aware, then you feel the subtle changes of consciousness that take place as each level is reached and are in tune with the consciousness to such an extent that you know the exact moment of release, or transference, as it is called. The moment of transference is too small to measure—it is instant. If you find yourself thinking: "I wonder if now is the right time," forget the whole exercise. Thought has no place on such levels, and if you can think, then you have not risen through the levels. Thinking is left behind on a mundane level.

The Safety Mechanism

Sigil Magick is the art of giving instructions to the subconscious mind in a way these will be accepted. Once accepted, they become fact. In order to do this we must bypass the normal conscious mechanism or conscious mind. This is accomplished by progressively silencing the conscious doubting mind in order to achieve an altered state of consciousness, thus allowing instructions to be given directly to the subconscious mind. It is for this reason that the subconscious mind has a safety mechanism which allows only specific kinds of instruction. Can you see the problems if every fleeting thought actually materialized? Unless you are a very positive-minded individual, you would not dare to lose concentration. Life would be madness for most people, and most certainly a trial for the rest! Ordinary thoughts are ignored completely but, using magical trance the instruction gets through. Shamanistic drumming tapes are ideal as a musical background for helping achieve magical trance and are available in a wide variety from most magical and new age suppliers.[3] You may also want to make your own tape recording of drumming.

---

[3]"Drumming for the Shamanic Journey," is an audio cassette tape distributed by The Foundation for Shamanic Studies, Box 670, Belden Station, Norwalk, CT 06852, U.S.A. Write to this address for this and other tapes. (I would advise anybody with epileptic tendencies to avoid using drumming tapes.)

Planetary Energy and Sigils

Magick is essentially very simple—robes, paraphernalia, physical temples, and so on are only useful aids. They help focus the mind, but the real Magick is done simply in your mind. An uncluttered, unfettered, almost childlike approach works well. In order to help activate sigils, you can use planetary correspondences to endow the sigil with the energy which represents the desire. For example: "I wish acquisition of my true magical power." This desire would come under the rulership of Neptune, who has countenance over Magick in general. This would involve setting the temple up using Neptunian symbolism. Find a quiet place where you can work undisturbed, and use something as an altar, a gray altar cloth, gray candles, Neptunian or Ambergris incense, your timing, and decide on how many rituals you wish to use and/or how many times you intend to "restimulate" the sigil in a ritual situation.

Making Sigil Magick Work

There are many reasons why sigil rituals fail to get results, and although it would be impossible to list them all, I will give you the main reasons in an effort to help:

1. It is vitally important that the intention of the ritual is thought about carefully before the sigil is created. It should be absolutely clear in your mind so that when you perform your rite there will be no doubts, uncertainties, and confusion to cause distraction.
2. While on the subject of distraction, there is little point in trying to work a ritual if half of your mind is occupied with the possibility of interruptions from other people. If you cannot fully concentrate on what you are doing, you decrease the chances of success. Do find a quiet place where you can fully relax and operate efficiently.

3. Pre-ritual relaxation is an absolute must. There is simply no point in trying to perform a ritual if you are feeling agitated, depressed, or desperate, or if your mind is still concerned with the problems of the day. Slow down, relax. Perform the "quickening of the subconscious exercise" (page 15) and then gradually bring your mind to focus on the ritual, not on the intention.

4. Get rid of unproductive thinking and unreal concepts, including all those unscientific absurdities such as: spirits, demons, and even the gods. These things are simply perversions of the art of contacting personalized forces from deep within the subconscious mind. Forget about purifying the temple; if it has been correctly constructed on inner levels it cannot contain evil or undesirable entities. Magick is a science, so treat it as such.

5. Not very long ago you could have been put in prison for being a magician or practicing anything deemed to be supernatural. If certain self-appointed guardians of the public morals had their way, this would still be the case. Fortunately it is not; however, secrecy is always a good idea, not because of the normal magical excuses, but simply because others may not agree with you. Minds are powerful things, so rather than risk blocks from other people, keep silent!

6. There seems to be a peculiar state of mind that needs to be adopted during sigil work in order to obtain a successful outcome. It is the ability to desire—not desire itself. You must take on an air of indifference, a could-not-care-less attitude. By consciously desiring a successful outcome, you may inhibit the natural process which will bring about the successful completion of your operation.

7. Imagination as a procedure is dual in nature. Its positive phase is one of creating and holding the sigil in the mind's eye, and its negative phase is one of letting go of

the sigil and not thinking of it any more after the ritual. This requires releasing from the mind the energy that has been generated. This is accomplished by dismissing the sigil from your conscious mind and permitting it to be released to the subconscious mind.

In the final analysis, a ritual is the end product of a great deal of thinking and planning; in addition, the more involvement on a personal level, the better it will work, for any ritual is a highly personal affair. After all, you are seeking to contact your subconscious mind. Instant potted rituals are simply ludicrous and, as such, unrealistic. The only ritual likely to have any impact is one that is fully understood, therefore it is always better to learn basic technique first, then begin to learn the art of constructing your own rituals in your own way. The works of others may well be valuable guides in some cases, but not always. Any ritual techniques given in this book are also valuable because you are given the all-important basic facts.

Creating Elemental or Magical Servitors

We will now learn how to work with elemental servitors to accomplish certain tasks. Servitors are entities with a certain degree of intelligence that are deliberately created by the magician. They are nothing more than components of the magician's personality which have been deliberately budded off from parts of the subconscious mind.

This type of magical operation is generally classed as *evocation* and equates very well with the pragmatic techniques in this book. The Law of Pragmatism is very simple: "If it works, it is correct." So do not be afraid of experimenting with your own approach to ritual work. Pragmatic Magick is primarily concerned with the use of magical techniques to obtain solid physical results, whatever these may be. All manner of important areas of life come into this category, including healing, restoration of self-confidence, money, success, love, and anything which necessitates "making things happen in accordance with the magician's will." With the use of elemental servitors, the magician can influence the mind of any other person. The magician can also cause changes in his or her own behavioral patterns and personality by improving intellectual faculties, removing bad habits and replacing them with better ones, and causing changes in the physical world.

There are three basic forms of magical operation: Evocation, where the magician sections off (or calls forth) an entity from his or her own subconscious or from his or her receiver's subconscious; Invocation, where a supernal power is called to indwell in a magician's subconscious; and Inner Plane Projection, otherwise known as Astral or Etheric Projection, where a transference of consciousness is made into the realms of the subconscious mind, in this case the Universal Subconscious Mind. The building of telesmatic images, creating servitors, ritual Magick, word-spells, healing, charging talismans, sigils, magical weapons, and even divination, are all variants of these three basic paradigms.

Creating Elemental Servitors

When the magician creates and empowers a servitor, he or she is creating an artificial intelligence capable of acting within a predetermined set of parameters that can be left to carry out simple tasks without any further effort from the magician. In order to do this, the magician must observe a few simple rules of conduct.

1. It is vitally important that the intention of the magical act is thought about carefully. The general nature of your working could be:

- Healing
- Divination
- Protection
- Luck
- Attraction
- Love
- Magical Attack
- Money
- Employment

These would then be used for a specific magical operation.

2. The specific nature of your intention is impressed on the servitor by sigilization. This is a magical technique whereby your intention is rendered into a graphic symbol. Of course this is not the only way. The magician can impregnate the servitor with the desire and the firm conviction that it will exhibit the wishes of its master—by thinking the command into it at the time of empowerment.

3. In order to give the servitor the power it needs to accomplish its task, you will need to assign the necessary symbols that bestow upon it the powers to act in accordance with your will.

4. The servitor has to be given a form corresponding to the desire the magician wishes it to fulfill. Using a humanoid shape is only one possibility; there are many others. You can use a shape which reflects the creature's bizarre functions, and, of course, the choice, as always, is entirely up to you. Servitors do work! So if you are going to use these, then build up some beneficial image, instead of subscribing to some primordial baroque entity of mischievous intent. Remember that in reality this creature is only a conceptualized autonomous creation. A common practice used by many practitioners is to shape an enormous morphic ball of light (or energy) in the appropriate planetary color/s in which the sigilized instructions or intentions will be impressed.

5. In true magical tradition, give the servitor a name. Everything existing, whether in a particular shape or shapeless, has a name. If it has no name, it does not exist.

These five basic rules are to be respected if the would-be magician intends to work successfully with elemental servitors. I will render the practice even more understandable by way of an illustrative example.

Creating a Healing Servitor

A friend who has recently undergone a serious operation is medically recovered but cannot seem to get back to his normal happy self, and life is becoming a misery. This is not normal as this friend is usually quite a happy person, full of life. Look at the situation in a detached way, then decide if a magical operation would help. If this is appropriate, which forces are appropriate and how do you formulate the instruction that forms the basis of your command? Also what about time? Do you want the servitor to be active all the time, or only work at specific times? For example, it could work every six hours for a period of six minutes at any one time. You could program the servitor to work at certain phases of the Moon, or when certain planetary transits occur that are beneficial to the magical operation. The servitor could be left dormant until it senses a certain condition which triggers it into operation.

As the problem is emotional, the general intent falls under the Moon—solving of emotional problems and response. Jupiter—joy and happiness—and the Sun could also be used, as the Sun rules healing and balance. You will need to incorporate these symbols into the servitor when it is being empowered, thus allowing it to draw on the power that these symbols represent.

Programming the Sigil and Symbols into the Servitor Form

When programming the servitor with its sigilized instructions, you can use a sequential method, whereby you visualize the sigil inside the servitor form, and then overlay any other symbols, lineal figures, and so on. If you are building a servitor with a specific shape, you can visualize the sigil at its core, almost as a strand of DNA, and then allow this to grow, forming a rudimentary nervous system and any other organs desirable. A reasonably clear picture will suffice. I have certainly not had any problems so far; i.e., all servitors I have empowered seem to have worked.

The Specific Intent

As you already know, sigils are made by fusing the letters of a desire sentence together to form a symbol which encapsulates your magical intent. First write down your desire in capital letters. All letters that appear more than once are omitted. The remaining letters are then styled into a glyph or sigil. The following is an example of a sentence of desire designed to promote recovery in the friend who has recently had a serious operation and who cannot seem to recover emotionally. As you can see from this example, the magician has fixed the time and duration of the operation and has expressed the birth and death of the servitor. Example of specific intention: TO RESTORE JAMES BROWN TO HIS FORMER HAPPY SELF, FULL OF JOY AND OPTIMISM. TO WORK AT SIX HOUR INTERVALS FOR SIX MINUTES FOR SIX DAYS. THE SPELL OF WHICH IS THE SUM OF YOUR LIFE. All repeating letters are omitted:

TO RESTORE JAMES BROWN TO HIS FORMER HAPPY SELF, FULL OF JOY AND OPTIMISM. TO WORK AT SIX HOUR INTERVALS FOR SIX MINUTES FOR SIX DAYS. THE SPELL OF WHICH IS THE SUM OF YOUR LIFE.

The above sentence reduces to: B K V C. From these remaining letters a sigil is formed. See sigilized desire in figure 6.

Assigning the Correct Planetary Forces to the Servitor

When the specific desire has been rendered into a graphic sigil, it will be necessary to assign to it the correct symbolic attributes which enable it to draw upon their power to accomplish its task. You will also notice that the number six has been used to good effect. This is the number of the Sun, and is associated with balance and healing. The following symbols were chosen to represent the qualities given to the servitor:

The Moon = ☽	The Sun = ☉
Jupiter = ♃	The Number = **6**

The symbols used to bestow characteristics and qualities on the servitor can be as simple or as complicated as you wish. Also, there are many ways in which ritual work may be enhanced. Color and scent help concentrate the sense of sight and smell. Color should be worked into the temple and the rites as much as possible; colored candles or lamps for the quarters; altar cloths and robes can be made in inexpensive colors. You can make or purchase one robe in a mutual color and have different colored sashes or cords for each rite. Robes are a good idea,

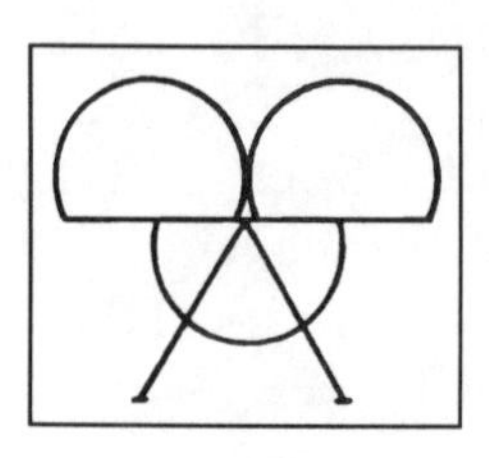

Figure 6. Sigilized desire.

as they help the transition from everyday life to inner awareness.

When you have completed your sigil and decided on which symbolic qualities you wish to give to your servitor, it will be necessary to render these into a complete symbol which will then be programmed into the servitor during the empowerment ritual. Complete symbolic instructions for this sigil are presented in figure 7.

Servitor Empowerment

Before any magical work can be done, it is necessary to calm the mind to make it more receptive. Anything likely to aid this is therefore valuable. Loud noises and other distractions can be quite a problem in the beginning. Eventually, you will be able to ignore these completely. When ready, perform the "quickening of the subconscious exercise" (page 15), followed by the erection of the Cosmic Sphere, and then enter the Inner Temple. Now imagine that at each of the four quarters there is a door or gateway which may be opened or closed at will. Open each doorway in turn, seeing the appropriate energy burst through—yellow at east, red at south, blue at west, and finally green at north. Having done this, we now turn our attention to the central pool. Look at the pool and know you are about to use power. If necessary, declare this in some positive way, like: "I now call on my never-ending supply of subconscious power." See the placid surface start to glow and effervesce and then burst into a fountain of power high into the temple, shimmering with energy and gleaming with light and power. The top of the fountain begins to bulge into a ball which draws the rest of the fountain into it. The magician contin-

Figure 7. Complete symbolic instructions.

ues to shape this enormous ball of pulsating energy, seeing it take on the color/s of the force/s it represents. When the magician believes that this ball of energy has reached its peak, the magician then names the servitor by speaking its name (say, CADULA), and impregnates this ball of energy with the symbolic instructions and attributes. The magician can then use a farewell gesture or think a farewell command such as: "So shall it be!"

You may like to use a martial arts' style "kiai" directed toward the servitor, such as "Hiiiiii." The technique is simple: you draw your hand up to your shoulder, as if preparing to strike someone; you then drive your will or energy through your arm, forcing it out through the heel of the hand as you quickly push your arm out. It is a short, quick punch, performed with the hand open, perpendicular to the wrist, fingers slightly curled. Imagine you are directing it toward the intended outcome. The servitor is then seen to shoot off into the microcosm, out of the roof of the Inner Temple. This should be done quite suddenly, severing the link between magician and servitor. You should then cease to dwell or think about the servitor; the more detached you are from the servitor, the more effectively it can operate. The servitor can then be left to work independently, free of any interference from the magician's mind.

These inner visualizations and methods are, of course, only suggestions; the fountain you ought to keep; the others could be changed in any meaningful way you feel is right. For instance, you could do away with the pool and fountain concept when working with servitors. I sometimes use an enormous ball, which I see burst through the elemental gateways; it pulses with the combined energy of the powers conjured. The servitor could also rush out one of the doorways, you could enter one of the doorways and empower the servitor, or because the intention falls under the heading of emotional problems, the servitor could be sent off through the western door, which corresponds to the Moon and emotional problems. There are many possible permutations. You must decide. The direction to work is easily found in Elemental Magick, and, as with the planets, you have to consider where each one fits in relation to the Encircled Cross. Table 1 (page 102) lists some practical suggestions.

When empowering servitors that have several characteristics and qualities there may not be any preferred direction, it all depends on the desired result. For healing wounds, for example, you could incorporate solar power and work toward Mars or south; for acquiring gold, this would depend on how you wish to acquire it. If you are looking for buried treasure, then work north; if you are unsure, then work toward the south, as this is the place of greatest light, or perhaps work toward the quarter in which the Sun is residing. In other words, in Spring—the east, in Summer—the south, in Autumn—the west, and in Winter—the north. Practice makes perfect, so study the planets, use the pool, obtain information, and rehearse your rituals.

Servitors can be used very well in seasonal rites (rites that are dedicated to each season of the year). The purpose could be attunement, learning, acquisition, or all of these. A ritual at Spring, for example, would be performed around the time of the Spring Equinox, and the aim would be the planting of an idea that would bear fruit in Autumn, and so on. This idea would be carried around the seasons at each of the four points of tidal change (i.e., the Solstices and the Equinoxes) by recalling the servitor by name, and rendering it more powerful with a new accumulation of energy. This method can also be used in conjunction with the lunar tides. This series of rituals uses the full cycle of the Moon, beginning at New Moon and continuing for approximately 28 days, using each of the phases in turn. There would be four rituals to be performed. The first is performed at the New Moon, the second when the Moon is at its First Quarter, the third at Full Moon, and finally the

Table 1. Planetary Directions and Cosmic Tides.*

PLANET	ELEMENT	DIRECTION	SEASON
Sun	Fire	South	Summer
Moon	Water	West	Autumn
Mercury	Air	East	Spring
Venus	Earth	North	Winter
Mars	Fire	South	Summer
Jupiter	Water	West	Autumn
Saturn	Earth	North	Winter
Uranus	Air	East	Spring
Neptune	Water	West	Autumn
Pluto	Water	West	Autumn
LUNAR CYCLE	ELEMENT	DIRECTION	SEASON
New Moon	Air	East	Spring
First Quarter	Fire	South	Summer
Full Moon	Water	West	Autumn
Last Quarter	Earth	North	Winter
SOLAR CYCLE	ELEMENT	DIRECTION	SEASON
Spring	Air	East	Equinox
Summer	Fire	South	Solstice
Autumn	Water	West	Equinox
Winter	Earth	North	Solstice

*In my book *The Magickian: A Study in Effective Magick*, you may have spotted an apparent contradiction in that I attribute Jupiter to the element Fire and south, and in this book I attribute Jupiter to the element of Water and west. The reason for this is that the sphere Jupiter—Chesed on the Tree of Life glyph—is Water of Fire. Jupiter rules Pisces (Water) and it also rules Sagittarius (Fire). In more recent times Neptune has also been given rulership over Pisces.

fourth is performed on the day of the Last Quarter. The exact time of these phases can be determined easily by looking in any ephemeris or almanac.[4]

Erect the Cosmic Sphere and enter the Inner Temple; as you have read there are four doorways inside. Each one could have a phase of the Moon on it, all you have to do is move toward the doorway that equates to the phase of the Moon being worked. Pass through the door, and you then find yourself in a room where you can call your servitor, in order to give it a new accumulation of energy. After this is done, leave the room and return back to normality. Close down the Cosmic Sphere. The next ritual is performed when the Moon reaches its First Quarter, and you change the inner symbology to suit. The remaining two rituals are then performed at Full Moon and Last Quarter. Again the symbolism should be changed to suit. These paradigms should suffice to give the would-be magician a paragon to create and work with elemental servitors.

Ritual Conditioning

Practice erecting the complete Cosmic Sphere and entering the Inner Temple, opening the four elemental doorways, and then meditating at the pool. This should be done for a period of 28 days. This ritual conditioning will help you acquire power; it will educate your subconscious mind to the fact you are going to use power. It is important to keep up the practice and not to skip any part of the program. You must get the idea of control to the subconscious mind, and you must also get to know where you are going to direct

---

[4]You can use Llewellyn's *Daily Planetary Guide, Astrological Calendar* or *Moon Sign Book,* for they all contain a general daily planetary and lunar aspectarian. You can also buy *Celestial Influences* calendars, by Jim Maynard (Quicksilver Publications). In England, *Prediction Magazine* contains a general planetary and lunar aspectarian.

this power. The balanced learning involved will take some time, so do not rush. There is no point in having power and not knowing where to direct it, so meditate, think, and discover. The pool represents your subconscious mind which contains all knowledge and also provides useful power. In Part II, The Cosmonomicon, you will learn how to attune the Cosmic Sphere and Inner Temple to the all-important planetary energies. Until then, you have lots of work to do building up what will prove to be a powerful psychodynamic base from which you can develop a realistic and highly effective magical system.

Part Two

The Cosmonomicon

The Ritual

7

The first six chapters of this book were designed to help put your magical work on a firm footing by showing you how to construct a sensible and powerful base from which to work: the Cosmic Sphere and Inner Temple. From now on you will be shown how to attune the Cosmic Sphere and Inner Temple to the all-important planetary energies. In order for this to be fully effective, it is vital that you fully understand all that has gone before and that you now be proficient in erecting the Cosmic Sphere and using the Inner Temple.

Although it is fashionable to adopt shortcuts or to engage in practices that belong under the heading of instant Magick, in reality there are NO easy ways to magical success. Naturally, some will find it easier to learn than others, for success hinges on many factors, one of these being the ability to unlearn the many erroneous ideas and concepts given to the novice by individuals or society. Do not rush. This is not a race to see who can be first past the winning post. Instead, take your time, learn, absorb, and work patiently toward your goal while letting others find their own pace. Speed is not the measure of success, and you would do well to heed the warning, "More haste, less speed." In addition, the input = output law is constant and invariable, so it is in your interest not to skip through preliminary work or perform your magical work in a half-hearted way. Little effort produces little result.

Let us continue to develop our realistic system of Magick by learning how to attune the Cosmic Sphere and the Inner Temple to those energies known as the planets.

Opening and Closing a Rite

This master ritual can be used for all manner of purposes. Bearing in mind what has already been written in connection with general ritual practices, any meaningful ritual should conform to this pattern of: 1) opening the ritual; 2) the main body of the work; and 3) closing the ritual.

A temple-opening ceremony may be as simple or as complex as you wish, providing that it is effective. All that you have to remember is that the opening ceremony is there for one reason only: to inform your subconscious mind that you are ready to commence magical work; in other words, you are about to change your thinking from mundane to magical. This may be achieved by using a simple opening formula which is followed by the erection of the Cosmic Sphere. You may use the following formula freely, for it is very effective with practice, or you may choose to vary it to suit yourself.

Opening Formula

We will presume that your workroom or temple has been set out for the ensuing ritual, and that you have spent some time relaxing and clearing your mind. Stand up in front of your altar and perform the Quickening of the Subconscious Exercise, then reach your right arm out in front of you. Imagine that a bright light is shining at the end of your forefinger, and that you can draw pictures in the air with this light. Use whatever means you can think of to fix this in your imagination, even if only for a second or two, as long as you are aware that it is there. This age-old symbol is the Encircled Cross of the Elements, and by constructing this in your mind you are putting your mind in touch with the elements in a rather special way. Do not worry if you cannot hold a vivid picture, this is not necessary, a brief glimpse will do. As you practice more and more, it will become clearer, and the habit of repetition will compensate for the apparent lack of visual. Say, either out loud or quietly in your mind:

From the center, flowing free,
comes all that is and will ever be.

See the light getting brighter:

Power on high, seeking direction.

Trace the upper arm:

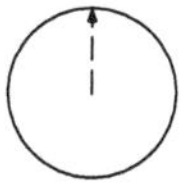

Power on Earth, complete perfection.

Trace the lower arm:

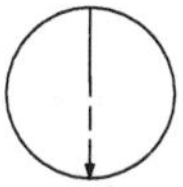

Right and reason rule the day.

Trace the right-hand arm:

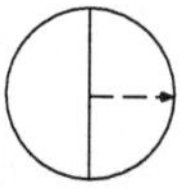

Love and order are the way.

Trace the left-hand arm:

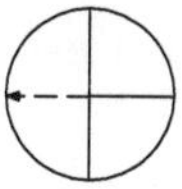

Round and round the wheel of light.

Trace the circle:

Endless power, shining bright.

Hands back at side. Light the central candle.

This opening formula is simple yet very effective if practiced often. It acts as an on/off switch which your subconscious mind will soon learn to recognize.

You will notice that there is a great deal of difference between this formula and the mumbo jumbo that the novice often associates with Magick, in particular the so-called words of power. I have already mentioned that any equipment used in ritual is not, by itself, magical. The same can be applied to words. There are no words of power as such, the power lies within the individual and your ability to use words as a tool. For a start, there is no point in saying words that you do not understand, such as Greek, Hebrew, or Latin. Not only will your subconscious mind not understand—you will not either! The golden rule is always: Never say or do anything that you do not fully understand. If you are going to use words, then for heaven's sake use plain English!

Use words by all means, but know what you are saying, and put some feeling and imagination into what you are saying. For instance, you could say: "Salve Raphael cuius spiritus est aura e montibus orta et vestis aurata sicus solis lumina." Or you could be more sensible and say: "I now open the gateway of the east," while seeing this in your mind and meaning all that you say. This makes more sense!

Having used the opening formula, it is now time to move to the second stage, that of erecting the Cosmic Sphere. First, erect the three rings in your imagination as described earlier (see page 59). Then enter the Inner Temple by the door in your imagination and direct your attention to the upper point, bring to mind all constructive ideas concerning god-power, and see the symbol of a jeweled crown. Now direct attention toward the base, bring to mind ideas concerned with Nature and the Earth-Mother, and imagine the symbol of a black cube. Direct attention toward magical east, see the yellow doorway of Air open, revealing the symbol of the Sword. At this point the eastern candle may be lit. Do the same with the other three elemental points in turn, seeing these open, each one revealing its appropriate symbol. The temple and Cosmic Sphere are now open and may be declared audibly, if so desired. You may now proceed with the main work, having established a fitting, cosmically correct basis for magical working.

I urge you to think long and deeply about this, as your creative mind can now function in a special way, and that way is called Magick. You control all that happens in this circle, in the same way that divinity creates a universe. The same laws apply to both, and both use the four elements to achieve that creation.

Eventually, when you are opening the Cosmic Sphere, you can do so all in the imagination. For the first year or so, practice it outwardly, physically, moving toward each quarter separately. You have to train your concentration into not breaking, and this is where all that regular practice comes in. Soon the whole procedure becomes automatic. When you have become proficient and fully fluent at opening the Cosmic Sphere, Inner Temple, and so forth, you should be cutting down on the words and gestures and speeding up the process. With regular practice you will be able to work the Cosmic Sphere in a shorter and shorter period. Certainly if you spend too long erecting the Cosmic Sphere and Inner Temple you are going to be bored to death before you get down to the point of the exercise.

With constant practice, you should be able to open the Cosmic Sphere with a single word or gesture. This is imperative on many levels, and once you can accomplish this and start applying it to everyday life, you will notice the most amazing changes beginning to happen. As soon as the Cosmic Sphere is opened you should feel *power*, not arrogance. Power is silent, it is within you. Notice that other people will see a change in you while it is going through you; it is truly extraordinary.

Do not worry, or place too much emphasis on getting the technicalities of the Cosmic Sphere and Inner Temple correct. I do not really think things out in a graphical, technical way. I just do what feels right to me. Sometimes when I perform the Inner Temple exercise the long-winded way, which I do from time to time, I play some meditation music or a Shamanic drumming tape, depending on my mood. I erect the Cosmic Sphere, then I perform the Inner Temple Exercise, but I remain aware that the Cosmic Sphere has been erected, but only on standby.[1] Of course I then bring in the use of the weapons. The point is, this method is really a beginner's way of erecting the Cosmic Sphere. You are in a huge room which could represent the Cosmic Sphere, then you have your four gateways where you are introduced to the four weapons.

I have never used physical pillars as such, they have always been in my mind only. I pass through the pillars, erect the Cosmic Sphere, put in on "standby" and continue. There is no sort of entering the Inner Temple as a separate exercise, for as I enter the room in use with my charcoal ablaze in one hand, I pass through those pillars and am already in the Inner Temple.

When I begin a rite the very first thing I do (in my mind) is pass through the pillars. Then I have entered my Inner Temple. The Inner Temple is a room in my mind where no one else can go unless I put them there. This room started off small, but just like my fountain, it has grown with me and is now quite large. It is just a room with four walls that are no particular color. Each wall has a doorway on which is suspended a weapon. When I am in the Inner Temple, I open the Cosmic Sphere; now all I do is see a line of brilliant white light above me, and a black one that goes below me reaching down to the cube. The top light reaches up to a crown; then, of course, I have the four ele-

---

[1]"Standby" means "ready for the work in hand."

mental lines of light, after which I erect the three rings, which I see as blazing white. They surround the whole of my actual house, which could explain why I no longer get disturbed while I am doing a rite.

This is all done instantaneously; it defies explanation. I know it is done though, because I hear noises in my head like things being slotted into place. If I do not hear that, I am not satisfied that it is done. Quite often this is accompanied by a feeling like a rush of energy, and a shift in consciousness sometimes takes place. All these lines of light emanate from my heart. The only important thing is knowing that they are there and trusting natural energy. The point is that your permanent temple is only a physical representation of the Inner Temple, so it does not matter, nor should it matter, where you are doing the rite, for Magick is of the mind, and it is what is going on in the mind of the operator that is important. So to sum up, you should be in the Inner Temple from the second that you start the rite.

You could use ribbons or cords if you really cannot visualize the beams of light. Perhaps it is because light is not really physical; you cannot pick it up or touch it. So use ribbon or cord of the correct colors. Do not struggle with it, after a while it will come easily, that I promise. With the Cosmic Sphere I do not think that you can put any percentage on it; different people can visualize at different degrees or percentages. At first it has to be a visual experience, and as you go along and get more sensitized to the energy that you are producing, it gradually becomes almost totally a feeling. Knowing that it is there is a matter of practice, persistence, and confidence.

I always try to work with as little paraphernalia as possible and now I just use incense. Some practitioners love having everything and turning a ritual into a major event; that is fine if it suits, but, more often than not, the rite becomes a psychodrama.

I have found that the subconscious mind must have a continual stream of fresh stimuli. Rituals work better if they are brand new, so think one up, work it out and rehearse it, perform it and forget it. Make a new one up for the next time. Before a ritual I usually make sure I know what sigils or symbols I want to involve, so that I have no difficulty with the imagination during a ritual nor do I get stuck for images at a crucial point.

If you have been practicing these techniques and feel confident enough, why not try doing a ritual or series of rituals with just incense, a Shamanic drumming tape, and just your own mind? You just might be surprised at the result. Treat it as an experiment. Do not take it as seriously as you would a full rite. Treat it like a packet of strange seeds you plant. You watch in awe and wonder as they grow, not knowing what they might be; yet when they are fully grown, they may be beautiful, not to mention rare!

The Cosmonomicon

From now on, all your magical work will be concerned with planetary energies. However, before we can proceed, it is necessary to define what these energies are, while, at the same time, attempting to remove the usual overdose of nonsense that attends most magical matters.

In the first instance: the planets, as such, do not have any influence whatsoever on human affairs, nor do they rule things of this Earth. The planets are symbolic in that they indicate a specific type of energy; for instance, Mars represents a person's inner drive and energy. The planet Mars cannot, by any stretch of the imagination, affect these things directly. I mention this only to clear up any likely misunderstandings which may have been created by people with little knowledge of the cosmic scheme. Each planet represents or symbolizes a certain type of energy. That is all.

Under the headings created by these divisions can be listed all manner of things, objects, circumstances, and so forth. In other words, everything in creation can be classified under certain specific headings, in this case the planets. The term "rule" is a convenient one. It actually means that a certain type of energy is akin to some object. For instance, Mars is said to "rule" the metal iron. The planet Mars does not affect this in any way; however, Martian energy has an affinity with this metal. The use of affinities is known as the doctrine of correspondences, and much use is made of this in all meaningful rituals. The main correspondences for each planet are given in the appropriate chapter. There are many others but these are omitted in favor of simplicity. As a student, you will no doubt find others, for this searching is part of the art; however, do take care not to accept all that is printed as being absolute truth. Many of these lists of attributes are, to say the least, erroneous.

It is always a good idea to work into the ritual as many of the appropriate correspondences as is reasonably possible. The reason is simple. These things are there to help concentrate the mind on the type of energy being used. They are not, in themselves, magical. Never forget the simple truth that these things act only as a focus for the mind, and nothing else!

The Sun

8

THE SUN	Planetary Glyph ⊙

Planetary Symbol: The Hexagram;
Color: Gold or yellow;
Metal: Gold or gold-colored objects;
Incense: Frankincense or any good quality solar incense;
Nature of the Planet: Healing, vitality;
Magical Ritual Uses: Gaining confidence; gaining fame; succeeding in gambling and speculation of all types; healing (both self and others); bringing joy into life; increasing personal stature; organizing abilities; pleasure of all types; increasing popularity; increasing vitality. The Sun also symbolizes gaining knowledge of the true self, and one's subconscious mind.

The lesson of the Sun is: whatever exists at the center will actuate at the circumference. In short, if the center is wrong then the entire structure is based on presumption and will therefore cause problems. The Cosmic Sphere is the effect, while the center is the cause. In medical terms, this we equate to the symptoms belonging to the Cosmic Sphere, while the cause of illness belongs to the center. You will notice that when medical science tries to cure the symptoms, naturally it fails. For instance, the Sun is at the center of both the solar system and the Tree of Life, and until the principles of the Sun and Tiphereth, as symbolized on the Cabbalistic Tree of Life, are understood and applied, nothing worthwhile is ever gained. Healing, which belongs to this planet, is achieved when the cause is cured, hence the magical use of solar energy. True healing cures by getting to the root of the problem, which exists as unbalanced belief and rifts within our own center. Once these are changed, cures quickly follow. In a way, it is exposure, for lack of a better word, to the energies existing within the symbolism of the Sun, that is bound to result in a gradual awareness of our own inner problems, and eventual healing.

The major correspondences and uses of this energy are listed on page 117. Study these carefully, so when you are faced with a problem which falls under this heading, you will know which energy to use. Let us now suppose that you are doing a healing ritual. The color to use is gold or yellow. This should be worked into the rite as much as possible, both outwardly, in the form of equipment, and inwardly in the imagination. Naturally, it is entirely up to you as to how you go about this, but here are some suggestions.

Incense. Use pure frankincense or any good quality solar incense which may be obtained from any good magical supplier. Incense is always a good idea, especially if it is well made.

Candles. Apart from the central and elemental candles, it may be a good idea to use additional candles as a focus; for example, to represent the person being healed. Use gold or yellow. Similarly, gold-colored candlesticks may be used if you can afford this.

Altar Cloths. It is quite normal for a magician to have a different altar cloth for each type of ritual. This can be very expensive. A far better idea is to have one main cloth, which could be white with, say, an Encircled Cross drawn on it, and then vary this by using a narrow strip of cloth or ribbon in the appropriate color. This may be laid across the center of the altar to good effect.

Altar Symbols. There is no need to buy a solid gold replica of Apollo or Bran; instead, use either the symbol of the planet or the planetary glyph. These can be easily made from cardboard and painted in the appropriate color. They should be placed on the altar where they can be seen, in such a way that they will not interfere with the ritual by getting in the way.

Attuning the Cosmic Sphere and Inner Temple. Having attended to the outer work, we now come to the essential part of the ritual, that of using the imagination in a rather special way. This inner work is seldom taught to students who are not initiated into a group.

Remember that you are dealing with solar energy, so the color is gold. Direct your attention to the upper point and see the symbol of the crown beginning to glow with golden light. Let this get brighter and brighter, and then see this light pouring downward toward you. Now direct your attention to the elemental doorways, starting at the east. See this golden light pour into the temple through this doorway. Do this with the other three doorways, in turn. As the light increases, see this play on the surface of the central pool. Now remember your intention and bring this to mind. Imagine that this thought is going into the pool; then see the pool turn into a fountain of golden light, rising higher and higher into the sky. Now imagine that these golden waters are pouring out through the four elemental gateways into the outside world. Finally, direct your attention to the lower point (the cube) and see this desire coming true, as though it were really happening here and now.

Imagine the circumstances or scenario you wish to bring about. Take your time over this, and above all else be positive: believe this to be true. After a suitable period of time, see the light fade and the fountain subside, leaving a calm pool once more. The main body of the work is now done and all that remains to do is to close the temple. This is done by simply reversing the procedure. Whereas the opening should be a slow and gradual process, the closing may be done much more quickly. Do remember that closing is just as important and should not be omitted. At conclusion, leave the temple or workroom and make any notes that you feel are necessary to your study.

The Master Ritual

Opening Formula—Part One (Encircled Cross)

From the center, flowing free,
comes all that is and will ever be.
Power on high, seeking direction.
Power on Earth, complete perfection.
Right and reason rule the day.
Love and order are the way.
Round and round the wheel of light.
Endless power, shining bright.

[Light central candle.]

Opening Formula—Part Two (Cosmic Sphere)

[Erect the Cosmic Sphere, then enter the Inner Temple. Just see a door with an Encircled Cross emblazed on it, pass through the door into the Inner Temple and stand before the pool. It often helps if you use words when doing this. You could say:] **Let the doorway to my Inner Temple be opened.**

[When you have entered the Inner Temple then direct your attention to the upper point and say:] **Behold the pinnacle of light embodied in the crown of the All-Father.** [See Crown.]

[Direct attention to lower point and say:] **Behold the fruits of Earth embodied in the throne of the Earth-Mother.** [See Cube.]

[Face East.] **Before me the doorway of Air,**
[See Door.] **opening to reveal the Sword of Light.**

[See Sword and light eastern candle.]
[Face South.] **Before me the doorway of Fire,**
[See Door.] **opening to reveal the Rod of Power.**

[See Rod and light southern candle.]
[Face West.] **Before me the doorway of Water,**
[See Door.] **opening to reveal the Cup of Plenty.**

[See Cup and light western candle.]
[Face North.] **Before me the doorway of Earth,**
[See Door.] **opening to reveal the Shield of Truth.**

[See Shield and light northern candle.]

I now declare this temple duly open.

The main body of work is now carried out. With practice your subconscious mind will obey your visualizations and realize that you are taking control of this power. This is also a good time to burn incense and perhaps consider your intention. To end the ritual:

Closing Formula

Let there be peace unto the east.
[See door close and extinguish candle.]

Let there be peace unto the south.
[See door close and extinguish candle.]

Let there be peace unto the west.
[See door close and extinguish candle.]

Let there be peace unto the north.
[See door close and extinguish candle.]

Let there be peace to the highest.
[See crown disappear.]

Let there be peace to the lowest.
[See cube disappear.]

I now declare this temple closed.
[Leave Inner Temple and close down Cosmic Sphere.]

Let there be peace all around.
[Extinguish central light.]

Leave the temple and write down any useful notes.

The Moon

9

THE MOON	Planetary Glyph ☽

Planetary Symbol: The Cup or Chalice;
Color: Silver;
Metal: Silver or silver-colored;
Incense: Jasmine or any good quality lunar incense;
Nature of the Planet: Response;
Magical Ritual Uses: Digestive complaints; domestic problems; emotional problems; female disorders; glandular problems; insomnia; pregnancy; self-protection; dealing with the public; the home and immediate surroundings; habits and mannerism. From an esoteric point of view, the Moon rules imagination and memory.

There are perhaps more stories, myths, and legends connected with the Moon than with any other celestial body. This is not surprising when one considers the inventiveness of human imagination and the fact that the Moon is our nearest neighbor in the solar system. In early days, ancient people could see only two manifestations of universal power, the luminaries—the Sun and Moon. When the Sun ruled, during the day, people worked, but at night they observed far more. They watched the Moon, noticed that it, like the Sun, appeared to move around the Earth, and that it also had phases. Gradually, it was observed that the tides responded to these phases and that seeds sprouted better during the Moon's increase. Women, who are naturally far more sensitive than men, felt these subtle changes and responded to them. With the passage of time and with the usual knack of presuming rather than thinking, the science of Magick became the worshipping of Sun God and Moon Goddess. There is a great deal of difference between the scientific use of the lunar tides and the meaningless hotchpotch now known as Moon Magick, so we will now look at the problems and the truth of the matter.

If you wish to gain control over those energies classified as lunar (or indeed any planetary energy), it is better to adopt the following plan of action:

1. Throw out unfounded beliefs and other misconceptions;
2. Learn how to attune to the planetary or lunar energy;
3. Adopt a sensible technique for directing the energy.

Clearing the Way

There is probably more rubbish written and spoken about the Moon than about any of the planets, and if your magical work is to be successful, it is vital that you reject this in favor of reality. Remember that whatever you accept without careful thought may well become a pattern of belief and as you know, belief gets results. It makes profound sense to accept only those things which happen to be true. For instance, you can, like many people, continue to believe that the Moon actually exerts some mystical effect on Earth. If you do, you will inhibit yourself and block your ability to be effective as a magician. It is far better to realize that, apart from the obvious magnetic effect of the Moon on the sea, or on plant growth, the Moon is not the source of some strange type of energy. In magical matters it is purely symbolic.

It really is quite amazing how people willingly accept a dogma that restricts or inhibits them. This is especially true in Magick. Take, for instance, the idea of the light and dark Moon. The light side is considered to be suitable for White Magick, while the dark side is allotted to works of evil or Black Magick. Do bear in mind that there is no such thing as Black and White Magick: there is only Magick. Without discussing this point at length, it is all a question of the intention of each individual. What is good for one person may well be evil to another. The truth is that each one of us must decide what is good or evil and act accordingly, rather than accepting the definitions of others. There are some good rules to follow such as: "Do unto others as you would have others do unto you." In other words, be yourself, act in whatever way you wish, and think as an individual, but try not to affect others adversely by seeking to deprive, restrict, or constrain them.

There are many great truths behind the idea of light or darkness, but to equate these with the phases of the Moon is, to say the least, stretching a point! Likewise, the idea of using the light side of the Moon for magical work and the dark side for meditation is self-limiting, and not in agreement with the laws which govern cosmic tides. Generally speaking, you can perform magical work at any phase of the Moon, unless you accept this restriction.

There are other unrealistic concepts, such as those which imply that the New Moon is good for beginnings. This may well be true for planting seeds but it is not necessarily true for you. The truth of the matter is that unless the New Moon forms an aspect to some important point in your birth chart, it will have little effect. This is also true of any other phase of the Moon, so do not waste valuable time waiting for the right phase. The chances are that you will not improve your magical work.

The Moon is said to rule the Olam Yetzirah, or Astral Plane, that strange place beloved of astral travelers, in which all manner of nasties and other undesirable entities are supposed to dwell. In the first instance, there is no such place as the Astral Plane. It is a condition of mind which belongs under the heading of imagination. Likewise, astral traveling is not really a form of movement by a detachable part of the body, it is simply another way of using the imagination to affect our subconscious minds. Although the experience of astral travel may seem very real, it is not real in the true sense of the word. What really happens is that the subconscious mind produces an accurate picture of some distant place and gives the illusion of actually being there. The experienced traveler does see these places quite vividly and makes the natural mistake of presuming that he or she has actually moved in a physical sense. The plain truth is that the subconscious mind is producing what can be loosely described as a three-dimensional television show complete with sounds, scents, and even atmosphere. Such is the power of the subconscious mind. It is also possible, not only to choose some predestined location but also to move backward through time, so that the traveler can experience past events. Some people make the mistake of presuming that this equates to a past life. Once again, there is no truth in this rumor.

Perhaps the greatest problem with all lunar Magick is that the Moon rules a powerful part of our minds—the imagination. This may be used to create, or it can be deceptive to the unwary. This is one reason why the so-called Astral Plane has something of a bad reputation and has given rise to stories of astral entities and illusions. These are nothing more than archetypal forces that exist within the deep-mind and the only illusions or deceptions are those which belong in the mind. Used correctly, the imagination is perhaps the most powerful tool at your disposal. Used wrongly, or allowed to get out of control by either daydreaming or believing in fantasy, it can literally run you around in circles. Your own Astral Plane (imagination) then becomes filled with all manner of fears and phobias which can easily be confused with intangible spirits, fate, karma, and so forth.

Attuning to the Moon

In order to make your magical work more successful, it is necessary to attune to each of the planetary energies. This is done by increasing your awareness of a particular energy, learning about it, and getting the feel of it. There are many ways to do this. First, you should look at yourself, in particular those parts of yourself ruled by the planet in question. In the case of the Moon, you should start by looking at the following.

Habits

All through life people acquire habits, some good, some bad. Habits are automatic reactions performed without thinking and have their roots in the subconscious mind. It is in everyone's interest to break bad habits, by first questioning them and then replacing them with better patterns of behavior. By doing this we not only remove what is essentially a restriction on ourselves, but we also open up channels along which better things may materialize. Take, for instance, the habit of negative thinking. People who suffer from this will face problems with a sense of defeat and despair, without really thinking about it. It is an automatic reaction, a bad habit, and unless it is replaced with a better habit, that of positive thinking, life continues to be a misery. The answer is simple:

change the habit. Once this is done, life is bound to be far more fruitful. We need to look at ourselves and our habits, question them, and then replace the bad ones.

Some habits are acquired from other people, and many are implanted when we are very young. One further group can be classified under the heading of repetition. It is a well-known fact that if we repeat something often enough, it is learned. In other words, it becomes habitual. Speaking, writing, walking, and using a knife and fork are some obvious examples. This can be made use of in the form of affirmations.

Before the educational system started to collapse, it used affirmations to teach children. One such example was the learning of multiplication tables or those little rhymes used to help retain important facts in the memory. One such example is: "I before E except after C." If something is repeated over and over again, it will be memorized. If we take matters a little further and repeat some statement with feeling and belief, this, too, goes into the memory, where it is acted on by the subconscious mind. This is the principle behind affirmations. Affirmations may be used to much better effect by improving the quality of our lives.

You can find ready-made affirmations in various mind power books; however, you can and should make up your own. This is quite easily done by first deciding what you wish to achieve and then putting this into a simple sentence. Suppose you want to become self-confident instead of being shy and filled with fear. Remember that shyness is a habit and that you are about to replace this with a better one. A useful statement would be:

Fear and shyness go away,
confidence is here to stay.

This statement may at first appear to be childlike and pointless. It is not. If repeated often (ten to twenty times) whenever you have time to spare and especially if said with conviction, it is bound to have an effect. The more you say affirmations, the better and more quickly the results will be seen, especially if these are repeated just before you go to sleep, for at this time your conscious mind is less likely to get in the way by presuming all manner of thoughts and concerns which have little to do with your intention. Use affirmations, they are a valuable tool.

Emotions

People with little control over their emotions are likely to achieve very little and are easily thrown off-balance by the slightest upset. Learn to calm down and control your emotions. Refuse to be impulsive and stop being touchy or moody. These things do no good whatsoever. They are bad habits and the sooner you are rid of them, the better for everyone, because you are damaging yourself and draining away energy in addition to annoying others. Sensitive people are easily molded by whatever comes along and inevitably used by other people. Remember that it is one thing to be sympathetic and understanding, it is another to be a crutch for those who will not help themselves because they are emotional without applying common sense.

Emotion is also a powerful magical tool, if under control. It is one of three. The power of thought and the use of the imagination are the other two. We have all seen what can happen when someone is determined or fired up. They are bound to succeed because the emotions are being used in a positive manner.

Learn to use your emotions like this. In other words, if you want something, be determined that you will have it. When using creative thinking, either during rituals or at other times, use your imagination to see what you want while adding the extra dimension provided by the emotions. Be determined and desire to have whatever it is that you see. There is nothing wrong with desire, so ignore those half-baked philosophies which insist that desires are evil and wrong. The extremists insist that all desire should be subjugated or done away with. This is not only silly, but virtually impossible. Any man or woman without desire is as good as dead! Desire is a powerful tool and it is perfectly natural, so use it. In addition, bring your feelings into your creative thinking by not only seeing what you want, but feeling that you already have it. This takes a little practice, but it is not as difficult as you may think. After all, it is quite easy to feel worried or experience fear when dealing with something that may happen. Change from negative to positive by learning how to control your feelings and then encouraging better ones, such as optimism.

It is a well-known fact that as you think, so you are. The same can be said about emotions and feelings. If your dominant thoughts are negative, then all manner of problems will beset you. If your emotions are also negative, this simply adds to the problem. The lesson is one of changing negative thinking and calming down the emotions. Learn to control these and your life (magical work) will improve beyond measure.

Imagination

The Moon is connected to our ability to use our imagination, and in the same way that the Moon reflects the light of the Sun, so our imagination is used to reflect pictures and symbols back to the subconscious mind. It is perhaps the most powerful tool we possess, yet it is only too often abused, scorned, or ignored. While there is little value in daydreaming (which shows the ability to imagine, but without any control), there is much to be said for dreaming. Dreamers are often urged to be practical yet, in truth, those who dream of greater things are inevitably the ones who attain such things. It was a dreamer (Edison) who gave us electric light, and it was dreamers who put humankind on the Moon.[1] Perhaps a better term would be visionaries, for they saw beyond the obvious and ignored the supposed obstacles. People of vision use their imagination to see what they want. They also use their imagination to provide answers to problems. The only difference between the ordinary person who muddles through life and a visionary is that the latter takes time off to dream of better things.

You may not be an Edison or a Ford but you do have the same tools at your disposal.[2] It is a question of widening your horizons, of thinking bigger, of dreaming of what you want rather than simply accepting life's handouts. Do not waste your time daydreaming. Exercise control by directing your imagination toward those things you would like to have. See yourself having them, indulge in your visions and make them expansive. Success comes to those who know how to use the power of imagination to predict the future by seeing what they want to happen and persisting with the vision.

Moon Ritual

Let us look at how we may increase our awareness of lunar energy. There are two ways to do this; first, by attending to the physical correspondences used in the temple, and second, by attuning the imagination along the right lines.

---

[1]Thomas Edison's inventions included the first practical automatic repeater for telegraphic messages, the gramophone, electric light, the carbon filament used in early electric lamps, and the phonograph!

[2]Henry Ford became interested in mechanics and experimented in automobile manufacture. He is famous for his V-8 motor, which he chose to build with the entire eight cylinders cast in one block.

The main attributes of the Moon are listed at the beginning of this chapter, together with some suggested uses for lunar energy. They should be worked into the temple in a similar way to that mentioned in the previous chapters. Take your time in planning your ritual, not forgetting to use your own ingenuity. It should also be noted that although silver is the metal of the Moon, you need not use real silver. It is the color that matters, so it is quite correct to use equipment that is silver-colored.

In order to complete the attunement of the mind, we naturally have to attend to the inner work of the imagination. This is quite easy to do although, once again, it does need a little practice before it is effective.

Use the opening procedure given in the Master Ritual (page 120), then burn some lunar incense (or jasmine-scented joss sticks). Let your mind consider the Moon itself; see this as a Full Moon shining down on the sea for a minute or so. In order to increase concentration, you may speak words that suggest you are about to use the power of the Moon. Here is an example:

> **I declare that the intention of this ritual is . . .** [state intention] **and I now propose to attune my mind to those energies which are ruled by the Moon. May the lunar energies respond to my will, turning needs into reality within the framework of cosmic law.**

Think about these words, do not simply repeat them. Direct your mind to the upper point and see the crown. Here, a useful variation may be used. Imagine that this crown has ten jewels set into it (one for each planet). Now see the silver jewel begin to glow, gradually getting brighter and brighter. Then say:

May those energies which equate to the Moon, flow freely into manifestations.

Direct your attention toward the eastern door or gate, and see this energy enter the Inner Temple as silver light. Do the same with the other three gateways in turn. You may, at each gate, say:

Behold the power of the Moon flowing through this . . . [name gateway] **gate.**

Direct your attention toward the central pool; see this glow with the same silver light and say:

Now do I direct the mediating influence of my subconscious mind to send forth this power into the world. May it go forth in peace harming no one yet overcoming all obstacles in order that I may have . . . [state intention] **.**

See the pool turn into a fountain of silver light. See this flow out through the four gateways and say:

Behold the power of the Moon now under the control of my subconscious mind.

Direct your attention to the base and see the cube glow with silver light. You should now spend some time in positive, creative thinking, seeing yourself having that which you desire and knowing that this is indeed about to happen. At the conclusion, close down as suggested in the Master Ritual.

Mercury

10

MERCURY	Planetary Glyph ☿

Planetary Symbol: Caduceus;
Color: Orange;
Metal: Mercury or brass;
Incense: Storax or lavender;
Nature of the Planet: Communication;
Magical Ritual Uses: For improving all nervous ailments such as absentmindedness; amnesia; anxiety; headaches; indecision; stammering; vertigo; worry; and so forth; for improving the mind generally, for example by better concentration; greater ability to learn; better speech and writing abilities; stronger nerves. Also covers installment payments, credit/finance agreements; brothers and sisters; contracts; coughs; education; gossip; slander; hearing; hygiene; interviews; intestinal troubles; letters; mail; lung complaints; memory; neighbors; relatives; rumors; theft; and transport (local and short distances).

The planet Mercury is symbolically related to our ability to communicate and think. It is this latter faculty, our ability to reason, that sets us apart from the animal kingdom. By this I do not mean that animals are inferior; I mean that the animal kingdom is governed by a different set of principles. The ability to reason, to analyze facts, to make decisions, to compare and evaluate, is unique to the human race. The ability to think belongs to humankind and it is the quality of thinking that determines not only what we become but also how the world advances. Thinking is a powerful tool and it is the responsibility of each person to use his or her mind in the right way. Failure to do so slows up advancement and causes problems of a personal nature.

There are many levels of thought: rational thinking, creative thinking, and original thinking. Creative thinking uses the imagination and best belongs to the Moon and to Neptune, while original thought belongs to Uranus. Rational thinking belongs to Mercury and covers such things as the ability to analyze, compare, evaluate, and synthesize facts. Naturally, people good at these things are classified as intelligent; if not, they are graded down. It is very important to understand that the word "intelligence" is often abused and misunderstood.

Society requires that we use our minds in a particular way, as decreed by prevailing trends. Our educational system teaches us to use our minds in an intelligent way, and is geared to the needs of society. Our minds are subjected to these needs whether we like it or not! If the aims of society are progressive and liberal, well and good (up to a point), but if they are not, as in an oppressive regime, then minds are educated in a restrictive manner to fit in with the plans of those who dictate the direction to be taken by society. Communism is an extreme example of how a society can enforce its limited point of view on others in order to survive. However, this is not the only example, for while it is easy to condemn obvious restrictions of this kind, we ought to also look at our own system of thinking or, to be more correct, induced thinking.

It is scientific fact that a child's character is molded during infancy. In this initial period, the child is educated by parents and by society. Add to this public education and you are likely to have a young person who thinks according to the needs of society. The child's ability to think is molded to fit the needs of society. Real thinking is discouraged because society is inflexible, needing to protect itself and the status quo. So, we have the odd paradox of society wishing to advance while it also seeks to restrict.

If we look at today's definition of intelligence, which is based on learning, we will see that this is little more than memorizing certain facts. The individual is examined, graded, tested. Intelligence is indicated by how well a person can memorize (or accept) facts presented in a school system. The point I am *trying* to make is simply this. If you were written off by society, or by the educational system, it does not mean that you are unintelligent. It simply means that you either could not memorize very well or, more importantly, you inwardly did not agree with the ideas that you were supposed to accept without question. There is hope for you yet!

Do not strive to be intelligent in the manner prescribed by society unless this suits you. Remember that most supposed intelligence is simply the ability to indulge in brainfeeding. Real intelligence is not about having a good memory; it is the ability to use your mind in a rational way by looking at the facts and then arriving at an independent decision about them. If only from this point of view, the educational system fails miserably.

The Great Misconception

Logic is a useful thing to have. Our logic and reasoning ability can quite easily be shaped to suit the system. Propaganda and media advertising are other examples of how the mass-mind can be molded. People are conditioned to accept facts presented by those in authority. From a magical point of view, there are two main problems: we are led to believe that 1) facts are unalterable, and that 2) stress and strain are the only way to get results in life. Both these ideas are wrong. They are misconceptions.

By using the mind correctly all so-called facts can be altered to suit the individual. Whereas normal practice is to look at life and then accept it in totality or give in altogether, the magical way is different. A magician recognizes that all physical objects contain energy and that this energy responds to the mind. Situations can be altered, obstacles surmounted, and events predicted simply by using the mind in a different way. Thinking influences things, it causes changes in direct proportion to a person's dominant thoughts. If these are positive, then good results occur; if not, then negative results are the order of the day. You cannot escape the law: "As you think, so you are." Change your thinking and you are bound to change your life. Remember that most of your thoughts, ideas, and concepts are not your own: they have been given to you by society. Changing your thinking is therefore largely a process of getting rid of preconditioned concepts (especially religious ones) and learning to think for yourself.

Stress is an unnatural phenomenon. It is totally alien to human beings. So why does it occur? Sweat and strain, rush around, do everything in a hurry. All these ideas are part of a fear of failure. After all, we must not fail, we must not make mistakes. As magicians, we realize that no one is perfect and that we all make mistakes. As a great thinker once said, "Life is built on a mountain of mistakes." It is quite permissible to make mistakes, it is another thing to keep on making the same mistake over and over!

Rushing around and living in a condition of stress will serve no purpose other than to burn up valuable energy and so it is wasteful. Slow down and remember the story of the tortoise and the hare. Learn to control your thoughts and actions and you will eventually achieve far more with considerably less effort. Take up the practice of relaxation and learn the art of letting go. Get interested in your mind and the peaceful way to approach life. You will never regret it.

Do you know what happens if you go to a doctor with stress symptoms? The doctor will prescribe a tranquilizer. Think about the word *tranquil*. It is the key to stress removal. The drug you are given induces a state of calmness and so you feel better. However, there is always the problem of addiction and side effects. By learning the art of true relaxation, you avoid the dangers of drugs and more important, you achieve the state of calmness essential to success.

From a magical point of view, you cannot perform a successful ritual in a state of stress, which is why you are asked to relax and push aside everyday thoughts before every ritual. This takes practice, because, as already pointed out, stress is now a way of life. It is not the way to success, especially in Magick. The more calm and tranquil you are, the better the result in every sense of the word.

The First Barrier

There is a barrier between you and the success that you so dearly need. This barrier lies in your mind, not in externalities. It is very easy to blame everything or everybody else for your own failure to be successful or content, but let me assure you that this is not the case. Once again, I must point out the truth. Your own thinking dictates what happens to you. Never blame circumstances: they are only being caused by your beliefs. This is most important. Look at your own thinking first. Ask yourself, "Am I being negative, do I expect little out of life, do I give up at every obstacle?" You may well be surprised at the answers.

Never blame other people. The truth is that they are only reacting to what thoughts you are sending out. If you are miserable, you will attract miserable people; if you are fearful, hurtful people will retaliate; and if you are convinced that you are a failure, the chances are that ordinary people will help you to become a failure. People always respond to you in the way in which you think.

The Problem of Intangibles

All manner of excuses are made for failure—and they are excuses! Perhaps the most odious is that of blaming something which is not there. Let me tell you a story to illustrate this point. Once upon a time, there was a wise and powerful man, well versed in the science of Magick. While he lived, his people prospered because he controlled natural forces in such a way as to ensure abundant crops, healthy cattle, and favorable weather. The people came to him with their problems and he advised them with great insight. They came to him with illnesses and he cured them. He was revered and respected by all.

Nearing the end of his life, the old man passed on the secrets of his Magick to a young apprentice so that people would continue to benefit after he had gone. The old man died and the younger, less experienced man took over the responsibilities of his master. All was well until one day his Magick did not appear to work. He racked his brains for the solution, often late into the night. The pressure grew as the people became restless. What was he to do? He could not admit that he had failed, the villagers would be very angry, nor could he carry on any longer trying to solve the problem. Suddenly he had what seemed like a flash of inspiration. The power would not respond to his will. Perhaps the power was tired of acting on command, perhaps it had a mind of its own, after all it was far more powerful than he. The idea began to grow in his mind until he wrongly concluded that the power had a mind of its own and that it now needed to be appeased in some way, just like an angry king who demands more taxes.

With his limited point of view he had built an image of something beyond his knowledge and that thing was about to become very sacred to him, because it gave him an excuse for failure. If his Magick did not work, it was the fault of something. So was born the absurdity of the intangible which was responsible for failure. This image, for that is what it amounts to, became an external entity (god, demon, spirit, etc.) which eventually needed sacrifice to appease it. It also gave birth to many other forms of absurdity, many of which are still with us and form part of everyday life.

It is very easy to blame fate: it cannot answer back! It is very easy to blame karma: it is beyond our control, or so they tell us! It is very easy to blame the stars: they are too far away to be questioned! It is very easy to blame God: after all, he DOES know best! It is very easy to blame all manner of things, providing that they are not there and if you do, you are believing the same nonsense based on excuses for failure put out by dogmatics! It is also a good manuever to avoid embarrassment for foolish and unskilled magicians, clairvoyants, and astrologers. Do not be fooled. There are no intangibles to blame.

The Mind as a Magical Tool

With Magick, you are dealing wth the science of using the mind. Start off on the right path by thinking carefully about your intention. There are several good reasons for this.

1. There can be no confusion later on because you will know exactly what you want.
2. By thinking about your intentions, you are bound to face certain doubts, uncertainties, and perhaps fears. Do not be put off by these things; instead, use your mind, apply

logic and common sense rather than giving up. Be positive and realistic, and realize that these uncertainties are not necessarily true. Realize and apply the knowledge that your subconscious mind can, and will, achieve whatever you wish, providing that you do not give way to the first obstacle.

3. The entire process of thinking deeply about your intention is bound to awaken your subconscious mind to the fact that you are about to give it an instruction. All of these thoughts are stored away in your memory together with the one fact that will ultimately make a world of difference. That fact is that you will eventually come to a decision. Your subconscious mind cannot work with uncertainty, confusion, or constant changes of mind, so a decision is bound to clear a channel of power ready for use later on.

Get involved with your ritual as this keeps the mind concentrated on the objective while bringing in the benefits of enthusiasm and excitement. Plan each rite carefully, decide on correspondences, do not forget to use your own ideas. A little ingenuity is far better than complete acceptance of established dogma or of some other person.

There is also the question of persistence. It is a commonly held view that one ritual will be sufficient in helping to achieve one's aims. This may well be true for an adept, but it is not true for the novice, unless he or she has the power of belief. More often than not, it is necessary to buffer the ritual in one of two ways. This is necessary in order to get around the habit of negative thinking which, although it may well be kept out of the ritual itself, may well cause problems later on.

Having spent a good deal of time building up to a ritual in a positive way, all too often the habits and pressures of everyday life start to block the channel of power you have worked so hard to open. It is important to keep this channel open by positive action or thought. As mentioned, this may be done in two ways.

1. Perform the same ritual at regular intervals, say, for a week or ten days.
2. Perform one main ritual, and then back it up with regular sessions of creative thinking.

Most of you will prefer the latter course for, apart from being simpler, the backup procedure can be done at any time. The value of the exercise is that it sustains positive thinking and helps your subconscious mind bring your desire to fruition.

The Power of Mercury

Mercury is the planet of the mind and so its energy can be used to enhance your mental faculties, or to remove problems such as stress, tension, anxiety, depression, worry, and so on. Look at the way in which you think. Is there room for improvement? Are you positive or are you negative? Do you worry, get depressed when things apparently go wrong, do you presume that life is predictable, or do you suffer from negative beliefs such as fate? Think about these things, they are important because it is your mind. Make a pact with yourself that you are going to be positive; you are going to better yourself by using your mind rather than letting it stay in a rut or be out of control.

Make a resolution that you are not going to put up with worry and uncertainty, that you are not going to be negative or give up at the slightest provocation. Be determined to regain control by taking positive steps to freedom of mind. You will never regret this. Once you have made this decision, refuse to waver. Keep in mind the obvious advantages and the vast potential available to you.

Use the power of Mercury to back this up along the lines suggested. Plan your rites, using the correspondences given at the beginning of this chapter. In addition, I would suggest that you make a list of your own problems. Think about these things, be honest with yourself and write them down. No one is ever going to see your list, so be frank. Make another list of the qualities of mind that you would like to have, such as decisiveness, alertness, calmness, and so forth. As you will remember, the act of thinking serves to stimulate the subconscious mind and pave the way for success. Magick is the science of using the mind.

Plan rituals to get rid of problems and bring about changes in your thinking habits. You can if you try, because your subconscious mind will always seek to cooperate with your wishes if you make the effort. In any case, the natural order of things most certainly tends toward harmony, peace, and abundance.

As a final point, stress results from being unnatural: in other words, from thinking, acting, and believing in a way that is contrary to life's true purpose. The thinking patterns you have inherited from society may well be in opposition to this truth. This results in an inner conflict which puts a strain on you and your peace of mind. Learn about life, use your mind, and resolve to discover the freedom that a well-ordered mind can give.

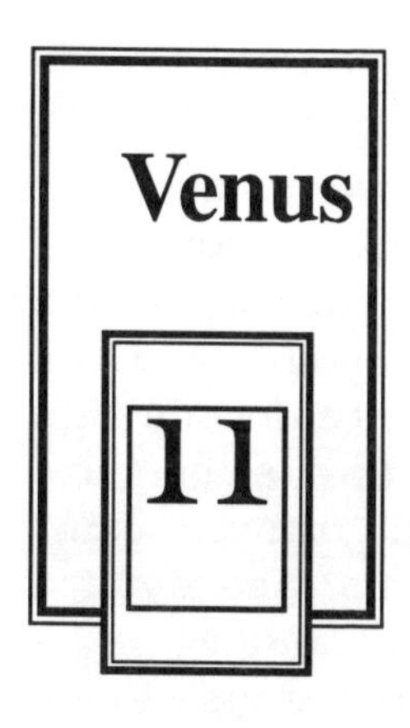

Venus

11

VENUS	**Planetary Glyph** ♀

Planetary Symbol: A Rose;
Color: Emerald green;
Metal: Copper;
Incense: Rose;
Nature of the Planet: Attraction, harmony;
Magical Ritual Uses: Gaining affection; associations with others; attraction to others; desires; earnings and earning capacity; finances and financial gain; income; love and love affairs; money; peace; pleasure; possessions; presents; the making of profit; relaxation; riches; social functions and success in this sphere; wages; wealth.

Now we will look at the power of Venus and how to use it correctly. Venus is the planet of love, beauty, money, and all things that can be classified as pleasant and desirable. Why is this? The myths associated with this planet apparently give little help in solving the riddle. Most people seem to know that Venus is beneficent but do not know why. It is the asking of the question "why?" that not only solves the riddle but also gives us access to the power of the planet through the understanding of its essential nature.

Have you ever thought about the word "nature?" Look around you at Nature, itself, and you will see the power of Venus in action. What, for instance, does the sight of the countryside conjure up in your imagination? First there is the obvious peace and tranquillity, you can almost hear the silence. Does this suggest inertia? No, of course not, for Nature is alive with activity. All around, birds and animals are feeding, breeding, and, in general, engaging in the task of living naturally.

Look at the way Nature goes about her business. She pours out activity, yet does this quietly and above all else, she is abundant. There are no restrictions on output, in fact there is excess. Any tree or plant shows this to be true. For instance, the real intention of any apple tree is not simply to look pretty or provide us with fruit; its prime purpose is one of propagation of self. Now look how this is done. The tree does not produce one or two prime specimens, hoping that this will be sufficient to keep apple trees on Earth; she produces hundreds of apples to make certain that apple trees continue to flourish.

Time and time again you will see this profound message if you care to look at life itself. A flower does not produce one seed; it fills its seedpods to overflowing. Most birds lay several eggs rather than one. The sea does not regulate fish to a few species; there are countless millions. Nature overflows with sheer abundance, and indulges in the law of excess. In other words, it is better to have too much than not enough. As you can see, when there is too much, Nature simply recycles the excess.

Human beings, as they grow farther away from Nature and from natural laws, ignore the profound, yet simple, message of abundance existing right under their noses. They try to create abundance by adding chemicals to the soil and by insane battery farming methods. The results? Waste and imbalance.

We cannot ignore Nature and survive, nor can we control or work with Nature until we understand the laws governing it. In this respect, science is stupid, but is this anything new? The only way to restore the balance is through harmony.

Venus rules Nature and Nature can teach us important lessons about its secrets and its energy. These are:

1. Peace and tranquillity are an essential part of life;
2. Abundance is natural;
3. Nature responds to cosmic energy patterns and thereby gains—so can you;
4. The natural way of life is through harmony.

The Law of Peace

You will remember from previous chapters the all-important equation peace = power. This is a natural law designed to help you attune to power and to help you see that power. No ritual or any other magical act is ever going to be a complete success until the would-be magician learns how to use the power of peace. Many try the alternative, some even succeed in deceiving themselves (and others), but few gain anything other than transient or shallow success.

Most people have an addiction to noise and they rush around as though there were no tomorrow. We are brought up with the idea that speed, stress, and strain are necessary if we are to succeed. This, however, is not true. Remember the old proverb: "More haste, less speed," or the equally prophetic story of the tortoise and the hare. These ideas are correct, as any truly successful person will testify.

Noise is perhaps the biggest affliction of the human race. People cannot seem to live without it. They have lost the ability to enjoy, and use, the power of silence. Put most people in a quiet room and they will feel uncomfortable, they will fidget and fret, and will be unable to sit still. Worse still, they may be afraid. Can you believe this? Afraid of something as natural as silence? In another vein, take away the idiots' lantern (television set) or the insipid cacophony emitting from a stereo system or transistor radio and some people are unable to function. Why? They have allowed themselves to be conditioned—virtually hypnotized—by noise. It has become a drug.

As the noise problem grows, more and more people will succumb to this way of life(?), not realizing that they are throwing away their entitlement to power. Noise will control them while other, more unscrupulous subcultures, will seek to control and manipulate behind the facade of progress. Day by day, the noise addiction grows and becomes part of life, and in the true tradition of "get to them while they are young," we now have the spectacle of children being spoon-fed disco music as part of their education. Naturally, these young people grow up needing this. The effect can plainly be seen in the rapid escalation of mindlessness and vandalism so apparent today.

Disco and pop music, by their very nature, breed disarray and violence. The whole effect is rather like a drug, and like all dangerous concoctions, ought to be put on prescription with severe limitations on its use. The accent is slanted toward destruction and so destruction becomes part of an individual's life if he or she accepts this as normal. Conversely, those who seek peace and reject the brainwashing from the media are still bound to reflect this in their lives. Disarray breeds disarray, while peace brings power; there is no other way.

If you would have power, you must seek peace. Do this by learning to relax the mind and body and by re-establishing your contact with Nature. Learn to look at your feelings in the same way that you should now be examining your thinking. If you are normally prone to depression, worry, uncertainty, vague feelings of unrest, and so forth, seek to replace these with optimism, well-being, and enthusiasm. Do not tell yourself this cannot be done. It can, if you apply yourself to the task. Become calm and cast your mind over happy events from the past or anything that will suggest happiness, be this real or imaginary. Get to know the "feel" of happiness. The feelings, like the mind, are a tool providing that you make use of these rather than letting them get out of control.

If you want lasting happiness and peace of mind, you must work for these things, not by struggle and strain, but by using the magical approach of calmness and control. Take particular note of how you react to life with your emotions. Do you have a bad temper? Do you blame everything and everyone else for your problems? How do you feel about circumstances and other people? These things are important. If your feelings are negative, then negative results will surely occur, so the lesson is again one of replacing the negative with positive feelings about life. In addition, as far as magical work is concerned, it is vital that you are not only positive in mind but positive in feeling as well. Know that you can succeed and be enthusiastic and optimistic about your magical work. If you do, you are bound to succeed when all other methods fail.

The Law of Abundance

Nature is abundant because she accepts the power of the cosmic tides without placing any restrictions on them. Human beings, who are in a unique position to understand these laws, and who also have the gift of a creative mind, normally choose to deny abundance and waste energy by adopting wrong beliefs.

Cosmic energy is never-ending and abundant. It can never run out or dry up, yet we have numerous idiotic concepts which seek to inform us that we must conserve or be cautious. While there is no excuse for sheer waste (or greed), it is a serious mistake to presume that our desires will not be amply filled. When we set up a thought pattern or belief, this has the effect of directing the subconscious mind to bring to fruition that which we desire. We cannot expect this to happen if, at the same time, we are applying restrictions. This only serves to confuse the subconscious or cause it to be cautious.

Let us take, for instance, the problem of money, or, to be precise, the lack of money. Venus tells us that we are like magnets, we can attract things (and people) into our lives. The problem is that we are already attracting all manner of things into our lives in keeping with our dominant thoughts (beliefs) and feelings.

Like Attracts Like

What do you really think about money? How do you feel about it? Be honest with yourself: are you positive or negative? The chances are that if you are mostly negative, you will get negative results. Let us look at the idea of money in some detail.

Right Attitude

What is money? Basically it is nothing more than pieces of paper and chunks of metal. Nothing more. It has no intrinsic value. Its value lies in the fact that it is simply a unit of exchange. In other words, $1 can be exchanged for one dollar's worth of goods.

What value do you place on a one-dollar bill? Do you simply see it as money which you must hang on to, or do you see it in terms of purchasing power? There is a world of difference, and it is essential that you see this. Money is potential; it buys things. There is no point in hoarding it, or trying to have heaps of dollar bills (or of any other unit of currency). This is the wrong attitude. It is not money, as such, that you need, it is the things money can buy that are really important. So when working rituals for money, always remember what you want the money for, otherwise you are simply falling into the trap of hoarding pieces of paper and metal. This has the effect of increasing insecurity, restricting your outlook, and removing the potential inherent in money. By all means work rituals designed to bring more money into your life, but do have a use for this, such as paying the bills or buying something special.

Money = Potential

One of the natural mistakes that the would-be magician makes is presuming that all life's problems will be solved by winning a large sum of money. The state lottery, or something similar, is the favorite target for attention. It is never a good idea to pin your hopes on this for a variety of reasons. In fact, if you are not careful, large amounts of money such as this actually cause a greater problem than existed in the first place. Your entire life style would change, but could you handle this? Would it really make you happy? These are important questions.

Always think before you start on a course of action and consider the effects that it may have. By this I do not mean that you should worry about it, or decide not to bother because you may make a mistake. There is nothing wrong with making mistakes providing that we learn from them, but it is a grave mistake to persist in thinking something into existence without due consideration.

Look at the possibilities. You could spend a great deal of time chasing the big win, and if you have sufficient powers of belief, you may eventually be lucky. Look, however, at the other side of the coin. You could be chasing money for no other reason than having it. There would be no other target. The chances are that, if you did win, you would soon find this a burden. Either you would waste it on unprofitable ventures or you would hoard it away, being afraid to spend it. The problem is that you would not have wealth consciousness. Wealth consciousness in this case means "the ability to stay in control," and it would not be developed due to the fact that not enough thinking has gone before.

By all means think in terms of large sums of money, but always have a use for it, such as building a business, buying a new home, enjoying the freedom of travel. Money then serves a purpose by helping you expand your life in meaningful ways. Money not only pays bills, it also gives you freedom. I should add that I do not consider winning competitions wrong; far from it, what is wrong is people's attitudes toward these things. Instead of enjoying competitions, people fall prey to a vague hope that prevents them from advancing in far more profitable ways. Concentrate on money, using Venus energy, but do have a use for it.

The Laws of the Cosmic Tides

All too often, the would-be magician has scant or imperfect knowledge of the cosmic tides. Hopefully, this book will assist in repairing the damage done by speculation or inaccurate postulation. That there are tides of energy can never be in doubt. The charting of these subtle influences belongs to the science of astrology: sensible astrology, that is, rather than the usual mediocrity so often presented to the public as the "stars." Evidence of these tides can easily be seen if you care to look beyond the obvious, or at least look a little deeper than normal. Take, for instance, the solar tides that create the seasons. Most people are only vaguely aware of the seasons, noticing that it is warmer in Summer or colder in Winter. To the magician, these seasonal changes are of great importance, or should be. On or around the Solstice and Equinox dates, the seasonal tides change quite dramatically. Individuals who are sufficiently sensitive to energy will notice this change quite distinctly. There are four of these alterations in energy flow. The first, known as the Spring tide, begins on or around the 20th of March, lasting until approximately the 20th of June, when the Summer tide arrives. This lasts until around September 20th, when the Autumn tide takes over. Finally, the Winter tide moves in around the 20th of December, continuing until the next Spring tide is due.

The seasonal tides form a background of energy patterns. There are many others, some noticeable, some more subtle. All can be predicted many years ahead of their happening using astrological calculations. This is possible by observing the movement of the planets against the background of the zodiac. It should always be borne in mind that the planets are symbols; that is, they indicate changes in energy. They do not cause changes. Returning to the Sun, it is not the Sun that causes seasonal changes; these alterations in energy would happen anyway and it is very important that you remember this. By observing the Sun's movements against the background of the zodiac, it is possible to predict when these tides will change. Exactly the same can be done with all other indicators of energy flow, such as the planets.

It would be a mistake to presume that the planets are the only way in which cosmic tides can be charted. There are bound to be others. For instance, anybody observing the sea could easily learn to predict the lunar tides without looking to the heavens. In fact one has only to look at Nature a little more carefully to see ample evidence of tidal changes. The reason is that Nature responds naturally to the tides. We humans, however, have a different approach.

Although we, like all living things, respond almost unknowingly to the cosmic tides, we do, however, have the distinction of being able to introduce an extra dimension into the equation, that of the creative mind. Whereas plants and animals respond almost totally to Nature and its energy flow, we humans can use the abilities within our minds in a special way. We can choose how we react and what the outcome will be. This single factor makes us the most powerful beings on planet Earth, if we but knew it.

We can use the cosmic tides to create whatever we wish in a physical sense, using the enormous power of Nature. It should be understood that the would-be magician does not need to be fully conversant with the intricacies of cosmic tidal flow, nor does he or she even need to know that these exist as such. The reason is that the subconscious mind already knows about such things. For example, think about using a calculator. You can easily use one to perform extremely difficult calculations with ease; you do not, however, need to know how the calculator works, or how to make one.

The ability to choose is our greatest asset, yet, so often, we are unaware that we have a choice, mainly because we have let others think for us. We believe and accept the most absurd conceptions, such as karma, fate, or the will of the gods, not realizing that these are untrue. More important, we constantly give up our right to free choice by listening to such rubbish and then accepting it as truth. Power, that is, real power, comes with the realization that we do have free choice.

The cosmic tides do not compel us or force us to conform. They are there to be used. It is not necessary that we undertake a prolonged and intensive study of the cosmic tides; this is best left to those who feel the need to investigate such things, using that branch of Magick known as esoteric. Our purpose here is a more mundane one, that of achieving physical results the natural way. In order to do this, all we have to realize is that cosmic tides do indeed exist, and they will, at any time, conform to the dictates of the subconscious mind. It therefore follows that if we instruct our subconscious, it will gauge the correct energies to use without any further effort on our part. All we have to do is give the necessary instructions. We must decide what we want, using our own free choice in the matter. The alternative is the inevitable cycle of problems, lack, stress, and ill-health that most people are now quite familiar with. This can be changed; all that needs to be done is to make a decision. In other words, make a choice between what is happening and what could be. Once that decision is taken in a positive manner, choice has been exercised and that choice *must* materialize, that is the law. We do have choices. Why not prove it?

The Law of Harmony

Venus is the planet of harmony. Why? What is harmony and how can we use it? Well, in case you thought otherwise, it is the natural order of things here on planet Earth, even if it does not appear to be so at first glance. All is as it should be, regardless of the supposed rights and wrongs. Let me explain.

To every action, there is a reaction; to every force, there is an equal and opposite force; and all that goes up must come down. You are all familiar with these expressions for they are well-known. In magical terms, everything conforms to the laws of cause and effect. This law simply states the obvious; for example, if it rains, then something will get wet! Put another way, if you exert force, say, in hitting an egg with a hammer, then it will break. This can be summed up as: force has effect. Why is this? The answer lies in the secrets of harmony, for everything has an equal and an opposite which seek to be in harmony. Physics says that every force has an equal and opposite force. Magick tells us that every cause has an effect; in other words, every force must have a result. The laws of harmony produce this result, one that is always in keeping with the nature of the initial cause. You can see this in the example of breaking an egg. The intention was to break it. In other words, you caused it to break. The result was in keeping with this cause: the effect was one of breakage. Were it not for the laws of harmony, as expressed in the principle of cause and effect, absurdities such as the intended breaking of an egg might actually result in a door closing, or even in a tidal wave! Fortunately, this cannot happen, thanks to the laws of harmony.

Thoughts are a kind of energy that have power through the mediating influence of the subconscious mind. Thoughts exert pressure and therefore get results. These results are always in keeping with the nature of the initial thought, again courtesy of the laws of harmony. Put another way, if you want to know what people really think inwardly, simply look at what is happening to them. It will be in harmony with their thoughts. Note that harmony, in the truest sense of the word, means an *exact* reflection, be this pleasant or unpleasant. If thoughts are destructive, people will experience destructive situations. Causes (thoughts) are being harmonized in like effects. Naturally, if the reverse applies, then better results are evident.

The laws of cause and effect, together with the laws of harmony, guarantee that we will experience or have everything that we believe in, for better or for worse. The cosmic tides do not differentiate between what is supposedly right or wrong for us. They seek only to comply in perfect harmony. In truth, terms such as "good" and "bad" apply only to human beings for we, and we alone, must decide using free choice. If we choose self-restriction, our subconscious mind will seek to supply it. Life energies will then comply with this intention. The reverse is, of course, equally true, but we each must decide what is right or wrong, good or bad. Think carefully about this, would we have it any other way? To do so would be to have life preordained and predestined. Would we really give up our freedom, especially now that we know the truth? Think about this, for free choice invokes the laws of harmony every time.

The Venus principle has always been linked to the power of attraction, to personal magnetism. It should be understood that Venus attracts both people and objects. Once again we must consider the laws of harmony, for what else is attraction but the *desire* for a harmonious result, whatever that may be. Desire is a force, especially if controlled and used. This may be done by using emotions and feelings in a positive way, rather than letting them stay dormant, or letting them run riot!

When you perform your rituals, put some feeling into your work, be enthusiastic and excited about the prospects instead of adopting the negative approach often advocated by so-called serious magicians. What is the point in wanting better things and going to all the trouble to study and apply this knowledge if you stand before your altar in fear of the gods? Fear is a feeling, and it is useless! Cultivate only uplifting emotions. Likewise, if you are going to speak words, then mean what you say. Once again, put some positive feelings behind them; you are bound to get better results. When using your imagination, do not sit there feeling gloomy or moderately hopeful; work up some desire; indulge in feelings of expectancy and anticipation. Be positive, feel good, feel confident, and be happy in your magical work. These may not be your normal habits, so if not, change them. Cultivate and practice positive feelings, for feelings, like thoughts, are powerful things if you choose to use them the right way.

Finally, do bear in mind that what you are inwardly as a result of your beliefs, inner thoughts, and habits is bound to have an effect on the world and the people in it. If you lack confidence, or if you are shy, even though you may not appear to show it physically, you are displaying this in other, less apparent ways. You are sending out signals, and these are causing a like response in others, for cause and effect never fails. The message is simply to look at yourself deeply, then discard those parts of yourself that are causing the problem. By doing so, you will change those signals and, of necessity, the response from other people.

Remember, Venus rules your power of attraction and it does not rule force, as in attempting to force someone to comply with your wishes. In all matters of personal relationships, Venus can enhance and quicken only that which is already there. Work toward love, not the attempted enforcement of love.

MARS **Planetary Glyph** ♂

Planetary Symbol: Pentagram;
Color: Red;
Metal: Iron;
Incense: Benzoin;
Nature of the Planet: Energy;
Magical Ritual Uses: Courage; powers of decision; self-defense; powers of determination; solving disputes; dealing with enemies; self-confidence; strength; vigor; virility; health (appendicitis, lowering blood pressure, boils and eruptive diseases, cuts and bruises, fractures, hernias, pain, rashes, scalds and burns).

Mars rules your ability to express yourself through the use of energy and activity. Negative conditions, such as tiredness, lassitude, and general low spirits may be worked on either magically and/or by using herbs and vegetables, such as garlic, nettles, cabbage, spinach, or non-toxic vitamin tablets containing iron.

The planet Mars governs energy, that is, the ability of each individual to express through action, as in physical exertion, acts of courage and daring, taking risks, and generally rushing ahead in life. In short, Mars equates to force. It is important to keep in mind that there is a right way and a wrong way to use force.

In olden days, the Mars force was the measure of success. Conditions dictated that this should be so, for life was governed by the survival of the fittest and ruled by those who were the strongest. Under the old tribal system, it was not the wise who ruled, but the man who proved by deed that he was a leader. Strength was the yardstick by which men were measured. The strong led, and the weak followed. In a way, human beings lived according to the rules of Nature, for experience had shown that it was better to do so. Nature decreed that only the strongest survive in order to perpetuate life on this planet and human beings, being very close to Nature in those days, followed its obvious lead.

Unfortunately, as time passed, people began to worship strength, and abused it in every possible way. Rulership became oppression and survival gave way to the need to conquer or slaughter anything or anyone who happened to pose a threat. As such, nothing has changed very much, for even today the power-mad maniacs seek to crush all that stands in the way of paranoid illusions of rule by obliteration. Naturally, might is met by retaliation and the whole sorry mess continues to lurch from one crisis to the next.

The correspondences of Mars are fairly obvious to understand. First, the metal iron became involved in Mars activities simply because it makes better weapons. An iron sword is harder and tougher than the bronze ones that preceded it. It takes, and holds, a better cutting edge, and, of course, only those with a higher degree of intelligence and technical ability can manufacture it. The Romans prized this metal so highly they actually used bars of iron as a form of currency. You can see examples of this in museums. Through the use of iron and the Martian qualities, the Romans conquered and ruled most of the civilized world. Unfortunately, the standards that they set are still being applied today.[1]

The color red belongs to Mars through two obvious associations: fire and blood. Early in our history, we learned to control fire and, as a result, enhanced our lives in many ways. The ability to control fire set us above the animals, and paved the way for greater things. With it we could cook, keep warm, drive away our enemies, and melt metals. We harnessed the power of Mars by using fire and so no longer were we afraid.

It is interesting to note how fire works, for it gives valuable clues as to the inner nature of Martian energy. If you apply heat to something, say, an iron bar, it will absorb the heat, gradually getting hotter until it glows red. What is actually happening is that the molecules within the iron bar respond to this heat by vibrating at a faster rate. As more and more heat is applied, the molecules continue to vibrate faster until they reach a speed at which their movement becomes visible: the metal appears to glow red-hot. The heating process is simply promoting more activity within the molecular structure. This shows Mars in action, for heat and activity are linked together and perfectly expressed by the color red. Think about this color, it conjures up ideas of warmth and energy. In its more negative aspect, how many times have you heard the expression "red with

---

[1]It is still mistakenly believed that the Romans civilized the British Isles and that prior to their arrival, the natives were little better than ignorant savages. Prior to these intruders, there existed a civilization far superior to any supposed culture that the Romans may be credited with. In fact, the truth of the matter is that Roman arts, music, philosophies, military tactics, and even gods, were stolen from others and then modified to suit the needs of the empire or the whims of its hierarchy.

anger," or "a heated argument"? The linkage of red, activity, and heat can be found in many areas of life. All are ruled by Mars.

The color red also suggests blood. This remarkable fluid keeps us alive by carrying oxygen and food to every part of our body. Without it we would die very quickly, a fact made use of by those who choose to use the negative aspects of Mars. Blood also played another important role in ancient times for it was presumed that certain qualities actually existed in blood. This gave rise to the idea of bloodlines through selective breeding. You can see remnants of this today in the breeding of livestock or in pedigree animals.

It was naturally presumed that if the headman was strong and courageous, these qualities lay in his blood. It therefore became essential that he mate carefully with selected wives, who also had virtues, in order that the children of these unions would continue to exhibit the same qualities, thereby perpetuating the powers of the leader. It should be emphasized that this type of selective breeding was not wholly limited to the perpetuation of the male line. Certain sects continued their lineage through the female, the male playing a secondary role. The aims, however, were different. In either case, people of the blood were considered to be rather special. In the case of the male (Mars-dominated) line, they were leaders, warriors, and men of courage who, through birthright, were chosen to lead others to an ever-increasing position of power in the world.

It is important to bear in mind that the power of Mars is a two-edged sword, it cuts both ways. Either we can use this power to enhance our lives, or we can make the same old mistake by using the more negative possibilities. For thousands of years, humankind has occasionally used Mars power wisely; more often than not, we have taken the apparently easier path of destruction. If we are to use this energy for the betterment of ourselves and others, it is essential that we look at certain facts.

Mars rules your energy and inner drive, therefore it needs an outlet. Energy is constantly being generated in accordance with your own metabolism. It cannot be stopped, it has to find some channel of expression, usually physical. Pent-up energy tends to force its way out unless it is allowed to find expression. Think about this. Are you active? Do you use energy, or does it explode at irregular intervals as bad temper or various degrees of violence? You must learn to control your energies, or they will continue to cause troubles. If you are restless and inclined to overdo things, you are not in control, and the chances are that you are doing more harm than good. The right way to control this is by learning calmness. Remember peace = power? This truth applies to every aspect of human life in addition to Magick, so learn to use it. Discover the benefits of relaxation, calmness, and a slower pace of life. "More haste, less speed" was not thought up to amuse people; far from it: it is an absolute truth!

Humans have been conditioned by society to believe that it is necessary to fight to the top, strive to attain things, sweat and strain to survive, and if necessary, trample all over others in the process. None of this is correct, it is simply a remnant of days gone by when people had to fight in order to exist.

Mars Behavior

Look before you leap; in other words, *think* before you react instinctively because your *instincts* (habits) may well be wrong. It is possible that these are conditioned reactions given to you by a society that still clings to the old standard of "might is right." Might, used wrongly, simply attracts even more might, usually as hatred and aggression. In any case, force is always matched by force, or, as the scientists put it, "to every force there is an equal and opposite force." This brings us to the second point.

The law of cause and effect *cannot* be avoided; only a fool thinks that they can escape from it. The wise person recognizes this law and *uses* it. How? Quite simply by seeking to use energy and inner drives in a way that is not aggressive, oppressive, or destructive toward others. If you truly wish to get on in the world, it is vital that you use the common sense approach of giving out that which you seek to gain. In short, "Do unto others as you would have them do unto you." This takes a little practice, but it does get far better results than the normal way of the world. Try it, what have you got to lose?

Aggression

Aggression is an ability that we all have, and like all things ruled by Mars, it is easy to abuse it, often without realizing it. Controlled aggression is a powerful tool in the right hands, and to use it correctly is not difficult. All that needs to be changed is the *direction*, in other words, the use to which it is put.

Decisiveness

Most people make no headway in life simply because they are afraid of making mistakes. This is a direct result of faulty education by parents and an educational system that insists on advocating the supposed fact that mistakes are wrong. Nothing could be further from the truth. No one is ever 100 percent correct; we all have, at some time or other, presumed that we are making the right choice when faced with a problem. If we are perfectly logical about this, our chances of being right are about fifty-fifty. Perhaps we choose wrongly; if so, we learn from the mistake and increase our knowledge. Be realistic. Life is built on a mountain of mistakes, so do not be afraid of being wrong. When faced with a problem, make a decision in the light of available facts, then stick to it. Do not dither, be decisive, and if mistakes have been made, we all learn from our mistakes.

Persistence

We need to learn persistence. We all can be stubborn or awkward, and this is persistence along the wrong lines. It is easy to give up, yet, if we care to think about it, we all have the ability to be quite stubborn about certain things. Having made a decision, we should stick to it until we succeed. Lack of persistence is probably one of the greatest causes of failure in magical work. All too often, there is an initial rush of enthusiasm then, as the time passes, the interest wanes. Naturally, with the passage of time, the age-old problem of negative thinking starts to creep into life once more, and so success is either delayed or even prevented altogether. We must ask ourselves if there is any point in performing the ritual in the first place if, having given instructions to the subconscious mind, we block the channels by losing interest. Perform the rituals and then persist in positive thinking by using creative thinking exercises to keep the channels open. Be determined that no matter what the obstacles may seem to be, we must succeed, or know the reason why.

With Mars, as indeed with all planetary energies, there is a wrong way to do things (usually the easiest) and a right way. All too often, the wrong attitude is applied when dealing with others who can be classified as the enemy. Once again, we are dealing with a conditioned reaction emanating from the past. First decide if the other person really is an enemy. How often has this mistake been made? Having established the truth of the matter, avoid the conditioned reaction of having a go or seeking to smash down the opposition regardless of the consequences! Stop and think. By reacting, we are in danger of escalating the problem and are wasting valuable energy. The situation can easily get out of control, resulting in more aggression, more hatred and even greater problems.

With Martian energy, control is essential, yet the temptation to react is very great and often seems justified. So what is the wisest course of action? It is often said that "prevention is better than cure" and in this profound statement is the answer to the problem. We must always remember that what we are, deep in the subconscious mind, determines what is likely to happen throughout life. An essential part of being a magician is getting to know ourselves so that any undesirable tendencies can be corrected. After all, what is the point in allowing bad habits to continue? All that they succeed in doing is bringing problems into our lives by virtue of the laws of cause and effect.

Reactionary habits, such as anger or the need to get even, solve nothing, for there can never be a real victor. Whoever loses will, deep down, start to resent it by brooding over it, or even hating the other person. Hate is a powerful thought form, and it can do a lot of damage to both the hater and the hated. Deep resentment and hatred can literally twist a person, mentally and sometimes physically, as well. The net result is misery, all because of a lack of understanding and a lack of control caused by conditioned habits. Is it worth it? The answer must be NO! With negative reactions, especially those involving Mars, there can never be any real winner, but there is a certainty that as long as they persist, everyone is going to lose.

I do not think people should allow themselves to be pushed around or abused by others. Everyone has the right to defend themselves and to be free from oppression. However, although we have been educated into thinking that we have to fight for freedom, history proves that this is not the case. Freedom comes to those who think freedom is the right way.

Bad Habits

By learning to control bad habits, such as hatred, aggression, bad temper, and violent reactions, you will be winning a far more important battle: that of self-discipline. Self-control means that you are projecting a far better thought pattern to the world and to other people, and so the net result is that others will be less prone to respond to you in an aggressive manner. "As you think, so you are." Can you see the wisdom in these words? By thinking peace, you will have peace; by thinking kindness, you will receive kindness; and by thinking strength, you will become truly strong. Looked at in this light, self-control does appear to be the best way, rather than continuing to allow instinctive reactions to rule your life.

Part of the art of learning to control the planetary energies lies in controlling yourself. With Mars, you must control energy and activity by ridding yourself of destructive actions and channels of thought. Resolve to acquire new habits and to think before you react. By doing this you will rechannel this power, and instead of wasting it, you will reap the benefits of self-control in many forms, such as self-confidence, calmness, decisiveness, inner strength, more energy, and better health, to name but a few. Each day, resolve that you will eradicate the following as best you can.

The Need to Argue

This simply blocks up the channels of communication with other people. They will avoid you.

Hatred

This burns up energy and can be proved to cause crippling illnesses to those who indulge in it. Hate breeds hate; there is nothing to be gained from it.

Anger

This, again, is a sheer waste of energy, which also damages health and causes a rift between you and those who could enhance your life. Anger is a negative way of asserting yourself. There are better ways, and leadership is one of them.

Violent Reactions

This is self-damaging, and worse still, it is quite possible to do something that you will regret. Violence begets violence, and it is rightly said that those who live by the sword shall suffer by the sword. In other words, the laws of cause and effect will presume that, since you think and act violently, you really want to suffer violence. Do you?

Resentment

This erects pictures in the imagination that are likely to affect your subconscious mind and produce the corresponding harmful reactions. There are two problems. First, cause and effect will bring problems of a similar nature; and, second, you are seeking to affect one or more persons on inner levels. Your thought patterns will be picked up on subconscious levels and others will, without necessarily knowing this consciously, seek to defend themselves, thereby giving you even more trouble. Brooding on supposed hurts serves only to aggravate the situation.

Uncontrolled Thinking

Without knowing the truth, people inflict all manner of ailments and misery on themselves due to their own thoughts. Let me tell you a true story of the effect of uncontrolled thinking.

> There was once a young man who decided to go it alone and start up a business. Night and day he toiled, gradually learning by his mistakes to become moderately successful. Because he had studied mind-power books, and considered himself to be quite positive, he never lost faith in his abilities even though, at times, things seemed quite desperate. During these times, he would stop, collect his thoughts, and then push out worry and other negative types of thinking until he had regained his self-control, and was thinking positively once more. The exercises proved to be valid and so his confidence grew and with it his business and earning capacity.
>
> All went well until he started to notice that certain items were not selling as well as they should be. In keeping with the faith-formula that had been his constant companion, he proceeded to put this right by positive thinking. This time, however, it did not work. In fact the situation got even worse! More positive thinking was tried, all to no avail. There seemed to be an insurmountable obstacle standing in the way, and his faith began to crumble until the day arrived when he decided to discover the truth instead of supposing or presuming.
>
> Looking for the truth, with any degree of sincerity, is bound to get a reaction because a decision has been reached. Once something is decided, the

> subconscious mind will seek to bring this to fruition, hence the importance of thinking carefully about your intention in magical work. Once the intention of the ritual has been thought out, a decision has been made, and that leaves the subconscious mind with a clear-cut direction to follow. It is exactly the same in life.
>
> That decision to look for truth had a dramatic effect, for within hours the truth did, indeed, make itself known. He suddenly realized that, deep down, instead of encouraging more business, he was actually driving it away. When he looked at his own thinking, he discovered that instead of being positive and inviting customers to avail themselves of his goods and services, he was actually thinking: "Please do not send any more orders, I cannot cope!" He was being aggressive by thinking: "I cannot be bothered with this anymore!"
>
> As you can imagine, this was quite a shock, especially as it happened to be true. However, once the realization was made, the results were nothing short of incredible. Business boomed and has gone from strength to strength ever since. The lesson is plain to see. If you are sending out aggression or antagonism, people will react to this and the tragedy is that it can all be done without a person realizing what is actually happening, because it is happening deep within the subconscious mind.

Aggression, together with other negative Martian traits, can be quite obvious, and easily recognized and corrected. It is also possible that some aggressions are buried deep within your subconscious mind, and may be working against you. In the latter case, it is so very easy to blame others or to presume that you are the victim of some form of psychic attack or other intangible, such as fate, or so-called karmic debt, when the truth of the matter is nearer at home. Before blaming others, look at your own thoughts most carefully. Look at the way in which you react to others and to life in general. Is this aggressive? Only you know the answer. If you are still uncertain, then ask your subconscious mind to give you the truth. Like the businessman, if you do ask, you will always get an answer. Asking is not difficult, for all that you have to do is wish to know.

From a magical point of view, there is little point in trying to use the power of Mars to defend yourself against all manner of insults, aggression, or even supposed psychic attack, unless you are in possession of the facts. You may even cause more trouble. First, seek the truth. Then act.

On a more positive front, the energies of Mars may be used very constructively to enhance your life in many ways by using the magical procedures outlined in previous chapters. These would, of course, be modified by using the correspondences of Mars. For example, when directing the attention to the upper point (crown) see a red jewel, use red light in the pool and fountain, and so forth.

It is a good idea to make a list of desirable qualities that you wish to have. Spend some time on this, thinking about it carefully. Do not forget to make another list of all the negative tendencies that you wish to remove from yourself, for it is just as important to rid yourself of these negative traits as it is to acquire inner strength. Having done this, you can then set about performing a series of Mars rituals in which you cover all items on your lists together during each rite, rather than being specific. General rules, like this, are just as valid, and pave the way for more precise work on a particular objective later on. All that needs to be done in the early stages is to plan a series of rituals to last over a period of time, say, ten days, in which you open the Cosmic Sphere and enter the Inner Temple, and using Martian correspondences, bring that power into the Cosmic Sphere and Inner Temple. Your intention would be one of making the best possible use of Mars within yourself. During the ritual, think about each negative point and see it leaving you. Push it into the pool and see it being washed away. Having done this, then concentrate on the positive qualities that you wish to have, using the fountain procedure to bring these into being.

JUPITER	**Planetary Glyph** ♃

Planetary Symbol: The Equal-Armed Cross;
Color: Blue;
Metal: Tin;
Incense: Sandalwood;
Nature of the Planet: Expansion, opportunity;
Magical Ritual Uses: Jupiter is the planet of expansion in all its forms and rules abundance; affluence; fortune; luck; prosperity; riches; wealth. Jupiter also rules long-distance communication; long-distance travel; legal matters; taxation; investments; higher education and academic matters; the deeper mind and all those who are in a position to help by providing opportunities.

In this chapter we deal with Jupiter, or to be more precise, the type of energy symbolized by this planet. Jupiter, along with that other beneficent planet Venus, has long been a favorite among students of Magick. After all, everyone prefers the "lighter aspects" of joy and abundance presented by Jupiter, as opposed to the more somber tones of, say, Saturn.

Jupiter is the planet of plenty—an everlasting supply of all things that are deemed good or joyful. Jupiter is the planet of *expansion*—limitless expansion, a fact which can either bless us or weigh us down with excess. In keeping with the optimistic outlook which Jupiter gives, not many magicians bother to consider both sides of this planet, or any other planet, if the truth be known. There are always two possibilities with any planetary energy: that which is positive and therefore beneficial, and that which is negative and therefore difficult. If a planet is considered malefic, like Saturn, the negative tendencies are quite obvious. In this case they would appear as severe restriction, hardship, and general inertia. As will be seen, this does not have to be so. Saturn has its good points, even though we often fail to recognize them. With Jupiter, the positive side is obvious, while the more negative traits tend to be ignored. However, it is important to consider these for, left to their own devices, they can often restrict our ability to derive full benefit from our magical work.

In truth, a planetary energy is neither good nor bad, positive/negative, beneficent/malevolent or any other division of opposites. It simply is. From then on it is all a question of our attitude toward this energy. This may seem a strange statement to make, having just said that Jupiter is a benefic planet. Well, it happens to be true. Look at what Jupiter represents or rules: joy, opportunity, luck, adventure, and so forth. You could hardly designate these as malefic, could you? No, of course not. We enjoy these things because they bring us happiness. However, the fact remains that it is our attitude to these things that really matters. We enjoy those things ruled by Jupiter, so, naturally, we look on the planet which bestows them as being beneficent. We adopt an attitude of mind toward the planet and all that it rules. The planet simply is. In truth, it remains a neutral source of energy, functioning along its specific channel and applying itself to those circumstances and objects which fall under its rulership. It is most important to remember this fact for, in later work, it will set you upon the right road toward more esoteric matters.

All planetary energy, although constantly outpouring, is essentially neutral. Only when it is modified by our minds does it become divided into good and bad. Our minds control everything, and we have the free choice to use energy wisely or with stupidity. "Good" and "bad" are manufactured in our minds, for there can be no such condition as neutral when dealing with power. Power is; we must choose the right attitude of mind in order to gain our heart's desires. Part of this process is, of necessity, one of looking at our attitude toward life and then ridding ourselves of those ideas not in keeping with our best interests. With this in mind, let us look at both sides of Jupiter with a view to gaining a balanced outlook toward its energy. The keyword for Jupiter is *expansion*. Therefore we must seek to work with this energy in truly expansive ways. How? Some useful suggestions follow.

God Will Provide

If you truly understand God, you will realize that God is an image. It is a well-known fact that the subconscious mind responds to images, especially if those images are personal. A perversion of this can be seen in spiritualism, where the medium communicates with supposed spirits or those who have passed over to the other side. They presume that they are actually in contact with disincarnate beings. I think that they communicate only with images, however real these may appear to be!

God does not provide, because God is simply a convenient image which we use to personalize power. The universe supplies the energy and your subconscious mind does the rest: for better or for worse, depending on your attitude to life and your beliefs. Jupiter rules beliefs; beliefs act as instructions to your subconscious mind which, in turn, produces physical results. The lesson is one of looking carefully at your beliefs, then throwing out the ones which are causing you trouble. A good idea is to begin by questioning any beliefs you have of God. After all, you will be simply looking at, and examining an image, an image which is probably not your own but one given to you by society and various religions. Many of life's problems are caused by fear of God and other related problems. So why not look at this aspect of your life, then build a better, more realistic image of God, based on truth?

Bad Luck

Many people believe in luck, especially bad luck. If something goes wrong, it must be the fault of luck. After all, some people are born lucky, others are not. This is what most people believe. Do you believe this? Remember: beliefs always get results! Then why believe in bad luck? Why be envious when you can also be lucky in life?

If people are lucky, they appear to get everything they desire; life is filled with good things, and there is no evidence of lack. Why? Is it because they are naturally lucky? No, not really. Everyone has the ability to attract into their lives whatever they desire. With some individuals, this is easy; it is quite natural. In fact, they expect this. Note the word "expect." Having seen these lucky individuals, did you ever take notice of their general demeanor or mental attitude? It is usually optimistic and very positive. They have an attitude toward life that, by its very nature, pulls in wealth and abundance.

So what makes you so different? Simply your attitude toward life and, of course, your beliefs once again. A lucky person feels lucky. What do you feel? Hopelessness, depression, uncertainty, doubts, fears? Do you presume that life will continue to drive you to an early grave, to deny you better things, to beat you down, to take away any chance of ever succeeding? These are beliefs—wrong beliefs! Truly lucky people are lucky because they believe in luck. It is quite natural to them.

Anyone can attract luck. It is all a question of changing your attitude from negative to positive, thereby effecting a change in circumstances. If you presume bad luck, you will have it. If, on the other hand, you realize that there is only neutral energy and your attitude toward it governs the type of effect that this energy will have on your life, then you have the key to the mystery of luck. Think, believe, and even presume that you will be lucky in life and it will be so! What have you got to lose? You can go on thinking that bad luck is the cause of your problems or you can think about luck in a positive manner.

Abundance

One of the best ways to get abundance flowing into your life is by believing in realistic concepts, such as the ones given in this book. Questioning beliefs, and even life, itself, is bound to open up your channels of power. Think and question, then adopt beliefs that are right for you. Part of the art of gaining success is to root out incorrect beliefs and replace them with better ones. Another useful technique is that of looking at your habits, then ridding yourself of those likely to restrict you.

Jupiter rules expansion which, in short, means abundance, good fortune, luck, opportunity, and sheer joyful living. By attuning to Jupiter and adopting realistic beliefs, all these can be yours. However, one other obstacle stands in your way, and this is the problem of negative Jupiter habits. What are these?

There is a great deal of misunderstanding about our place in the universe, and in particular, our role here on Earth. Certain wise people did try to point out the way of things, but their words were twisted by bigotry and hypocrisy. We are conditioned (and I do mean conditioned) to believe that the material side of life is evil. We are advised that we must evolve away from the material; we are told that physical being is the lower rung of a ladder that we must climb to spirituality. This is a misconception. However, the problems caused by these concepts are still with us and often materialize in subtle ways.

Taking In

Each one of us takes in energies and uses these according to our needs, or so it should be. Our ability to use these energies successfully is entirely dependant on our beliefs, and if those beliefs are wrong, then it naturally follows that the results will be undesirable, varying from disappointment to a complete catastrophe! With Jupiter, we are dealing with our ability to use the principle of expansion in all its forms. It should be remembered that we have this ability and we can use it. However, if our attitude toward life is wrong and our beliefs are colored by absurdity, we will then restrict the flow of Jupiter energy into our lives. Jupiter rules expansion and this implies abundance. Therefore, lack of abundance is entirely due to wrong beliefs, particularly the ones inculcated by religious dogma and to a greater or lesser extent, contemporary esoterics.

If you believe in evolving by rejecting the material side of life, you will know only lack. If you presume that God is out to punish you for your supposed sins and that you must redeem yourself, you will know only lack. If you believe in fate, bad luck, and other absurdities, you will know only lack. If you continue to accept that the obvious is unchangeable, or that life must continue to be the way it is at present, you will know only lack. Do you really want lack?

In addition, Jupiter-related problems are due to wrong beliefs. Among these are: greed, overindulgence, squandering, carelessness, complacency, exaggeration, gluttony, religious difficulties, and legal problems. All of these are caused by a lack of understanding of life. How can, say, constant legal problems be the result of wrong beliefs? Well, if we look at a birth chart, the position and aspects to Jupiter will tell of benefits and problems likely to occur in that person's life. Contrary to popular opinion, there is no compulsion in the cosmic scheme, and it is nonsense to speak of fate, destiny, and inevitable consequences arising from the planetary positions and aspects in a person's chart. A birth chart is simply a measure of potential. If Jupiter is well-aspected, there is a tendency to luck, optimism, and lots of useful opportunities in life. This is not due to luck, but to the ability of the person to make use of Jupiter energies in beneficial ways. Good aspects simply mean an easy flow of energy. If, however, Jupiter is under difficult aspect, then the reverse will tend to apply, and there is a greater likelihood of the more negative tendencies entering into the person's life. Again, this is not due to bad luck, but to wrong usage of energy.

To return to legal problems. All legal matters are ruled by Jupiter. Therefore, if a person has difficult aspects to Jupiter in the birth chart, there is a strong likelihood of legal complications. Fools may put this down to karma or fate, but this is not the case. The real problem lies within that person's mind as a negative Jupiter belief pattern. Like attracts like and so the effects of this are bound to manifest as problems. As far as the individual is concerned, life seems harsh and there seems to be no way to avoid the difficulties. It is then very easy to believe in fate or even the will of some god. Naturally, beliefs such as these will do nothing to alleviate the problems, they will probably make things worse!

If you truly wish to change your luck and have abundance pour into your life, you must change your beliefs.

How? Not by using critical self-analysis, although this may appeal to some, but by simply adopting new beliefs. No matter what the aspects may indicate in your birth chart, these can always be used to enhance your life, even though they may have caused you considerable difficulties in the past. A difficult planetary placement or aspect indicates that you are inclined toward unsuitable inner beliefs, resulting in negative Jupiter-type problems. In short, the abundant, expansive nature of the energy will be providing the wrong sort of abundance, owing to the fact that your subconscious mind is simply seeking to carry out the instructions given to it. It knows nothing of right and wrong, good or bad, or any other type of moral distinction; it only understands instructions (beliefs), regardless of how these originated. Remember that most of your beliefs, values, standards, moral code, and so forth, are not your own, but those given by parents, teachers, relatives, and society in general. They were accepted by you when you were quite young, before your power of discernment had developed. You believed what you saw and heard; in short, you trusted all that was presented to you, and then allowed this to fade into memory. It was forgotten, yet it became habit. Think back, how much of your life is ruled by those early days? Has anything changed, have you altered anything, have you thought about these values? The chances are that you have not, so they continue to work.

I mention this simply to point out that most of our thinking is preconditioned and is nothing more than an extension of the thoughts of others. We do not really think only within the confines or beliefs given to us since birth. Naturally, a heavily afflicted Jupiter will suffer more than most, for it tends to attract and absorb more of the negative possibilities. Likewise, the well-blessed Jupiters will be the ones who are supposedly lucky in life.

To change your luck or to attract more abundance is therefore a matter of replacing old and outmoded beliefs with better ones. This is not difficult; in fact it is remarkably easy, providing you make the necessary effort. Here are some practical suggestions.

Changing Your Mind

Keep the truth constantly in mind. Think about it often, and accept it as a reality: it is. The real truth is that Jupiter energy, like all others, flows constantly. It can never be exhausted or depleted; it is eternal and everlasting, it is neverending, and it is freely available at all times. You may be using this energy in the wrong way, or not to its best advantage, nevertheless you are in constant contact with it at all times. Your beliefs shape this energy; they give it form in physical terms. Your beliefs shape your life, for better or for worse. You are not fated, nor are you subject to karma or the will of some outside entity or intangible force. You have free choice. This is the only concept that makes any sense for, like it or not, you are using free choice if you really care to think about it. You choose to accept the beliefs of others instead of thinking for yourself, and although this can be excused in early life when you are more trusting and somewhat gullible, it is time to exercise choice once again. Unless you do, nothing will ever change, and life will continue to appear to be beyond your control.

Power of Abundance

If the power of abundance does flow freely into your life, then all you have to do is provide a more fitting channel along which it may flow. There is an old truth that says you cannot think of two things at the same time. Try it; you will find that this is true. Make use of this fact by regularly using affirmations. An affirmation is simply a phrase or sentence which epitomizes some essential truth or new belief pattern. This is repeated often until it is learned by the subconscious. You can see how this works if you cast your mind back to school days and the techniques used in learning multiplication tables and other necessary pieces of information. These were repeated over and over again until they were memorized; that is, until they were accepted by the subconscious mind.

Affirmations

Using affirmations is really quite easy and well worth the effort involved. First you must think up some suitable phrase which sums up your intention, be this better health, more money, self-confidence, or anything you like. As we are dealing with Jupiter, a suitable phrase could be: "With each passing day, I allow Jupiter energy to bring joy, opportunity, luck, and overflowing abundance into my life."

Say this often, whenever you have spare time, especially first thing in the morning, before the pressures of the day begin, or last thing at night before going to sleep. It is not sufficient to simply repeat words and expect miracles. In order to get the full cooperation of your subconscious mind, you have to put feeling into these words and use your imagination. How would you feel if abundance did flow into your life? Try to capture this feeling, see yourself having all that you desire, and try to be optimistic during this exercise. In short, indulge yourself in this brief excursion into the reality of subconscious instruction.

Affirmations may also be ritualized to some degree. This does not mean that you have to perform a full-scale rite with candles, incense, and so forth. All that you need to do is find a quiet place, spend some time relaxing, and then, in your imagination, erect the Cosmic Sphere, finally repeating your affirmation slowly and deliberately as indicated previously.

Ritualized Affirmations

Regular ritual work with the energy of Jupiter is bound to be beneficial. Either use this energy for some specific purpose or, alternatively, adopt the intention of opening up to this power. By this I mean allowing it into your life so that it may, guided by your subconscious mind, begin to work for you. Keep the intention in mind; use an affirmation such as: "I allow the beneficial energies of Jupiter to enter my life in accordance with truth and the laws of abundance."

Use the appropriate correspondences, both physical and imaginary. See the bright blue light flood into the Inner Temple, bringing with it joys of sheer abundance, and once again, use creative thinking to assist in building a channel along which this power may flow into actuality. Remember, life really is trying to give you everything that you desire. All that you have to do is allow this to happen by providing a channel. Even the slightest effort will be repaid.

Giving Out

I mentioned earlier that there is the two-part equation of taking in and giving out. There are many ways to look at this. It makes no difference if you are a magical practitioner or not, you are bound to mediate planetary energies. In other words, you take these in, and through the incredible abilities of your subconscious mind, you direct these to cause physical effects, even though you may not be aware of this fact. Magick is the science of learning to understand and use the power of the subconscious mind so that the giving out attains more favorable results. Magick gives you control, providing you take the time and trouble to learn and apply knowledge. Therefore, by self-discipline, realization, and application, you learn to give out planetary forces which carry your intentions rather than fears, or vague hopes and wishes, and the effects of negative belief patterns.

We can also control what we effectively give out by seeking to adopt a little-known cosmic fact. For the purpose of illustration, imagine that you act as a pipeline through which power flows, rather like water flows through any normal pipe. Your beliefs will not alter the rate of flow, they will simply color the effect. However, your actions can, and do, prevent a fullness of flow. In effect, it is possible to choke this flow by adopting bad habits in keeping with the negative side of a planetary energy. For instance, with Jupiter, the habit of greed will effectively block your own access to abundance. Negative Jupiter habits act as a brake, they slow up the power flow. The lesson is one of taking a good hard look at yourself and then, in the light of honesty, resolving to get rid of the problems you see. In addition, to help restore the flow, do the reverse. This means learning how to give. You can see evidence of this in truly abundant individuals. They give out, they are generous and beneficent to others. As you give, so shall you receive. This is the law and furthermore, it works! Think about this, then apply it, not for selfish, egotistical reasons, but for the simple reason that by doing so you are conforming to the laws: the law of abundance and the law of cause and effect. Seek to give and you will gain, often in surprising ways.

SATURN	**Planetary Glyph** ♄

Planetary Symbol: The Triangle;
Color: Black;
Metal: Lead;
Incense: Musk;
Nature of the Planet: Limitation;
Magical Ritual Uses: All business matters; delays; land dealings; oppression; cultivation of patience; endurance and stability; professional matters and one's profession; property; self-control; ambitions and career; personal security.

There is always the temptation, when dealing with Saturn, to let its somewhat sinister reputation color our thinking. After all, the word Saturn is not unlike Satan who, in turn, is hardly representative of beneficence and kindness. To the uninitiated, Saturn is a rather drab, lonely planet represented by Father Time, who never smiles, nor does he appear to have anything to do other than plod along, getting older and more tired with each step. Saturn is blamed for all manner of unfortunate occurrences and, like its metal (lead), it seems to weigh heavily on our souls. Although it cannot be denied that there are problems with Saturn energies, these are mostly avoidable and their overgeneralized malefic reputation is not fully justified on close examination. Let us now examine Saturn's energies in a realistic light.

Saturn is the planet of *stability*, and any form of stability must represent restriction of one sort or another. What kind of mad world would we live in if there were no stabilizing influence? It would be impossible. Without gravity, we would float off into deep space; without friction, nails and screws would simply fall out, car brakes would be ineffective; without wind resistance, an arrow would never stop. The Saturn effect certainly has its uses, if we care to look a little deeper.

Part of the problem concerning our fear, or dislike, of restriction is due to a misinterpretation of the laws of the cosmos. We have for countless centuries been led to believe that life was a restriction in itself. We were given gods who apparently had a purpose for us which inevitably implied that someone or something out there had decided what our future must be, and how this should be best governed. How silly! We were also given the most appalling laws which, apart from bearing no resemblance to reality, gave us an overabundance of negativity. In short, we learned that the laws were absolute, and that we could do nothing about them, so we had better learn to comply. The matter is all the more sad because the entire concept was, and still is, inaccurate. People began to expect the worst, so naturally they got it! As you believe, so you are.

Cosmic laws are there to be used, unlike the civil laws based on a need to inflict fear and oppression on people. No cosmic laws exist other than to be creative and to aid creation. This is the absolute truth. Problems arise by wrong usage of these laws which, in turn, are caused by wrong beliefs. It is not possible to live without cosmic laws. The absence of laws gives rise to disarray and there can never be disarray in the creative scheme. All is in precise order; all is perfection, and all is as it should be. "How can this be true," you may ask, "when there appears to be so much trouble in the world and so many things that are wrong?" A good question, but you should already know the answer.

Given that the cosmic laws are true and that they are unwavering in their action, given that the subconscious mind always responds to our beliefs, given that the subconscious produces physical effects which are always in keeping with these beliefs, is it not true that ALL is really perfect and as it should be? Think about this carefully. You believe, using your own free choice to do so, therefore you are responsible for the physical effects which surround you. In truth, you are getting perfection. Your subconscious mind is providing exactly what you believe to be true. All is therefore as it should be, it cannot be any other way. Matters change only when you change your beliefs. In which case, your circumstances will automatically change to suit this new directive and you will, once again, have a perfect result. Creation creates with great precision and total perfection and you have the power of creation by using your mind to direct life energies according to your desires.

Perhaps we ought to look a little deeper at the supposed malefic tendencies of Saturn. There are many, the main one being that Saturn is a tester of humankind. The idea that Saturn (or its gods) represents a tester for humankind is absolute rubbish, and came into being as a result of misguided and muddled thinking. If we are to presume that the Creative Spirit conceived and then created man and woman, why on Earth should it need to test him or her? Test for what? Surely the all-knowing, all-seeing, all-perfect God would know what it was giving birth to in the first place?

The idea of testing humans is an old one which was born out of apparent necessity. After all, if you were about to elect a new tribal leader, that person would have to prove that they were the best. No one wanted a weakling in charge, for this could lead to all manner of catastrophies. Kings and priests were tested to see if they were capable of shouldering the responsibilities of their office. Unfortunately, this became the norm in the wrong context. Evidence of this can be seen in lodge initiations in which the candidate is subjected to various ordeals.

The testing of our fitness to enter a spiritual state of existence has become the backbone of monistic and dualistic religion and an integral part of contemporary esoteric thinking.[1] This misconception is based on our supposed "fall" from grace, and has resulted in all manner of strange dogmas such as karma, reincarnation, and of course, an overwhelming belief that the material world is evil. None of these concepts are correct. Karma is the result of dogma gone mad; reincarnation, as a compulsive cycle, has no basis in truth; and the material can never be classified as evil. The material world simply is. It is our reaction to and our manipulation of the material world that is the real cause of trouble.

It is very fashionable and trendy to deny the material side of life in favor of a more spiritual outlook, but you are urged to think about this carefully. The material can be troublesome—not because it is evil, but simply because it responds to our thinking. If our thinking is wrong, then the physical effects are wrong, and although it is natural to blame physicality, this solves nothing. It is equally pointless to blame circumstances for these, too, are manufactured by thinking patterns rather than so-called fate. Those who try to deny the material, or consider it to be evil, are deluding themselves and causing a great deal of self-suf-

---

[1]The dualist believes God to be separate from His creations, whereas the monist holds that God is present in all things; but a "fall from grace" is particularly Christian and, even though Christians take on other traditions and practices, they frequently see the "other practice" through Christian eyes.

fering. Beliefs always get results, and for these individuals the physical side of life will tend to be barren and unproductive. Worse still is the mass effect on human thinking as the prophets of this form of unreality try to inflict their views on others, usually succeeding in their efforts.

Perhaps the greatest guide to the reality of life, especially its physical existence, is the Cabbalistic Tree of Life. All too often, would-be magicians use this symbol, yet fail to recognize the emphatic message that all energies impact on Earth and find their fruition therein. Our role in this is simply one of exercising free choice to use these energies as we will, according to our understanding and knowledge. The Tree of Life may certainly teach knowledge that is spiritual in nature, but it also teaches practicality—a fact that is missed by most students and teachers. The Tree of Life does not imply compulsion, coercion, or self-restriction, and so it is with life. If only people would realize this!

Saturnian Fear

The problems of Saturn do not belong to the planet or its energies; they exist in our own minds as misconceptions and wrong ideals. These are inherited and accepted without thought, causing all manner of problems. Let us look at some obvious examples.

There are two types of fear: that which is essentially self-protective and therefore useful, and that which is based on preconditioning around the needs of society. We all have a fear mechanism; it protects us in times of danger by giving us strong sensations and certain bodily chemical reactions. This type of fear is quite natural. Without it we would be unable to recognize and react to danger. The other type of fear is completely useless, being based on intangibles.

For example, our normal fear reaction moves in when we are faced with obvious problems—such as a hooligan with a gun or a falling rock. We see the danger and then our fear mechanism warns us of the danger. This type of fear is selective and therefore useful. On the other hand, negative fears work largely in the imagination as a result of the conditioning given to us by society, religion, parents, and so forth. They are irrational and largely unfounded, rather than being based on probable fact. People spend vast amounts of time indulging in fears and phobias (such as the fear of spiders) to the exclusion of reality. It is rarely realized that, apart from being nonproductive in real terms, this sort of fear can actually do a great deal of damage, because it is a belief pattern. Normal fears move in when something is actually happening; negative fears pray on the mind and are concerned with possible circumstances rather than actualities. There is little point in fearing what may happen. It is far better to use creative thinking and to be positive, because there is always the danger that fears may come true.

Be rational about fears. Are they justified or are they speculative? If the latter applies, then throw them out of your mind quickly. Think about your fears, face up to them, and have the courage to question their validity. You will be surprised at the results. If you would be a magician, fear is one of the first things you must beat, especially fears such as the supposed effects of fate, karma, or the will of the gods. Defy these idiotic ideas, challenge them, and subject them to the light of scrutiny. Why believe in fate and nonexistent gods? These absurdities can rule your life if you let them, even to the point of preventing success altogether. Is it worth having such fears?

Negative Thinking

Fear and negative thinking are based on presumption rather than fact. Once again, it is a result of the conditioning given to each of us by society. We learn to think negatively almost from the moment we are born. It becomes habitual, so we do not notice it. Look at the way you face problems, especially your normal reactions. Are these positive, self-assertive, and confident, or are they negative? Do you shy away or run from troubles; do you hide in a corner? If you do, does it solve anything? The answer is no. In order to gain, you must be in control, so retreating is simply valueless. In any case, what are you running away from? An actuality or a presumption?

In Magick, negative thinking can prevent success without you knowing it, which is why you are urged to spend time in regular sessions of creative thinking after a ritual. Creative thinking keeps the channels of power open and helps you beat down those negative thought patterns. Use it!

It is a true fact that the way we think determines what happens to us. This is the absolute truth. If our dominant thoughts are negative, then we receive the same from life. It can, and does, become a vicious circle. We start by being negative which, in turn, creates negative problems, generating even more negative thoughts as we presume the worst and so on ad infinitum. Once the simple fact is grasped that a negative approach gains nothing, then the cycle is halted. Naturally, better results occur, but you have to make the effort in the first place.

Dealing with Facts

In this world, we are taught from an early age that facts are unchangeable. This is rubbish! If you are going to become a pragmatic magician then you have to reject this idea. Acceptance that the facts cannot be changed is a pattern of belief. We all have this belief, and sooner or later we have to throw it out in favor of reality. A wise magician looks at the physical facts, sees them as being obvious, and then realizes that the physical is composed of matter and energy. Energy can be controlled by the subconscious mind, and the physical can be altered or made to respond. Extreme examples of this can be seen in telekinesis, in which physical objects are made to move around by pure thought.

The facts may well speak for themselves, so we are told, but the plain truth is that these facts were created by minds, and if this is true, then they are not real in the truest sense of the word; they are transient and therefore alterable. Perhaps the easiest facts to alter are those that are not strictly physical. Take, for example, the fact that your earnings are not sufficient for your needs. There is an element of presumption in this. At any time, those earnings could be boosted to realistic levels simply by believing that this will happen. You do not attempt to alter this week's pay; instead, you alter the future projection by using the "butterfly effect," which states it is easier to bring about a small change in the universe than a huge one, but that enough microscopic fluctuations will generate macroscopic diversity over time. There is quite a difference between the two approaches, yet, all too often, the would-be magician attempts to influence the present facts instead of the possibilities. Once something is factual, it is difficult to change. The easiest way to change is to determine what the future will bring, rather than allowing things to continue as they are. This is one of the real secrets of Magick. Use magical techniques to change the future, as yet unmanifest, by analyzing when and where to "nudge" the unfolding event; then you have a powerful key to the mysteries of abundant living.

The alternative is to accept things as they are or try to alter something that is already in existence: not an easy task! There is a great deal of profound sense in the statement that prevention is better than cure. So it is with Magick. Projection is better than prolongation. Seek to change the future rather than the present or the past.

The more positive side of Saturn becomes obvious when one considers its nature. Saturn is the planet of solidity and stability, both of which are essential to life. If there is power, the power is useless unless it can attain form. Saturn gives form through its stabilizing influence. Without the Saturn principle we would all be composed of formless energy in an equally formless universe. What a boring thought!

Saturn Energy

Using the energies of Saturn is no more difficult than using the power of any other planet, providing that the now predominant negative ideas are cast aside. Some of these have already been discussed, but there are other problems. Saturn rituals may be used to alleviate the following:

Responsibility

There is nothing wrong with responsibility; in fact, we cannot avoid it. However, it is quite possible that we are taking on far too much out of a sense of duty. Do ask yourself, duty to what? Must we bind ourselves to it to the exclusion of personal happiness? The answer is no. In any case, you can do too much for others. Not only will you be used, you will also act as a crutch for people who cannot, or will not, help themselves. Help others by all means, but do keep a sense of perspective and balance. How often have people thrown away their entire happiness and personal advancement because of some sense of duty to another person or to a cause? Their reward? Wasted opportunity and a pat on the back. The alternative could have been much more beneficial to all concerned if common sense had been allowed to rule the matter.

Depression

This is fast becoming a modern disease thanks to the efforts of a medical profession that prescribes drugs rather than common sense. We all get depressed but there is only one solution: get rid of depression! It is an acceptance of negative thinking to a chronic degree, and if allowed to continue, it is bound to influence your future. Kill it stone-dead, now! By far the best solution is to break the pattern which caused it. Too much work, too much worry, too many problems. Get out in the fresh air, change your routine, and fill your mind with optimism rather than despair. Go into the silence of your mind, discover the peace therein, and spend time casting your mind over pleasant events—whether from the past or pure inventions. Learn to relax (it is a marvelous tonic) and remember the truth about life.

Worry

Despite the fact that most people are now addicted to worry, it solves nothing. In fact, it can only add to your problems and help ruin your state of mind and your health. Worry implies uncertainty. As a magician, you have to develop the positive side of yourself. This means learning to be certain. Instead of indulging in the uncertainties of worry, stop, relax, and bring the mind around to creative thinking. Worry is a habit: change it.

Loneliness

There is a great deal of difference between the natural need to find seclusion and peace, and shutting out the world and other people. Often there is a deep-rooted belief that other people may hurt victims of loneliness and so, to prevent this, these victims retreat into themselves without realizing what is actually happening. The cure for loneliness is to make a positive effort to make contact with other people, and to drop what is, in effect, a lack of self-confidence. Creative thinking can be used for meeting others and gaining the resultant happiness that this is bound to bring.

Death Phobias

Contrary to popular opinion, Saturn is not the planet of death. This properly belongs to Pluto. The idea of the grim reaper and other idiotic concepts were given to us by certain religions. There is nothing to fear about death, for it is a natural process that we must all face. Some people fear retribution which has been inflicted on us by dogmatic fools and, incidentally, is still perpetuated in various forms by today's esoteric teachers. There is no retribution, nor are there penalties or places of divine torture, such as hell. When you pass from this Earth life, you return to the peaceful state that you came from. You are not made to pay for your sins.

• • •

All in all, Saturn is a beneficial planet, despite its supposed malefic reputation. Meditation on its energy and its nature will reveal much to those who concern themselves with such matters. Use the planet: it is part of you and it is your friend. Remember that, "As you believe, so you are." In other words, if you allow the more negative tendencies of Saturn to rule your life by believing in such things, this will color your life accordingly. Far better to use it constructively, not only to remove negative belief patterns, but to help achieve your aims. Saturn aids those who are ambitious and seek to consolidate material goods. This is the real purpose of Saturn

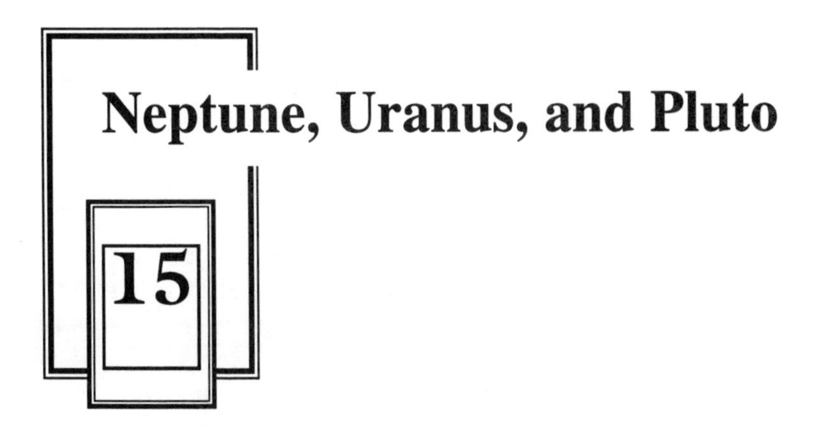

Neptune, Uranus, and Pluto

15

In this final chapter we will look at the three remaining planets: Neptune, Uranus, and Pluto. These are known as the outer planets, and were discovered relatively recently. As a point of interest, it should always be remembered that energy is without end, it has always been in existence. As every type of energy has its physical correspondences, particularly in the heavens, it naturally follows that Neptune, Uranus, and Pluto have been with us for a very long time.

It is important to get to know each planet. Any good astrology book will be a valuable source of information. The more familiar you are with a planet, the better your understanding and subsequent ability to use the energy the planet symbolizes. The same rules apply to Magick as to life: knowledge aids success and the acquisition of knowledge requires patience and study. There are no shortcuts and once again, the input = output law holds good. Look at it this way. If you wanted to succeed at being a mechanic, you would seek practical experience in a factory and perhaps take a course that leads to gaining a diploma or other qualifications. You would not pick up a book, read through it quickly and then seriously expect to design or repair an engine. Of course not! Yet many a would-be magician attempts to do this with Magick and is surprised when the results are not forthcoming.

There is no substitute for individual effort, especially in Magick. If you wish to succeed, be prepared to work for success. Also, never let others do your thinking for you. Knowledge is the right of every individual and you already have this knowledge within your own mind. Only individual effort, discovery, and realization are of any worth. Of course much can be gleaned from the writings and examples of others by applying your own critical faculties. Ask why. Question everything until it reveals the truth. This is the only path to real knowledge.

The alternative is to conform to the dictates of others, regardless of whether they are right or wrong. Very few people bother to think. They let others think instead. What a waste! Look especially at the modern esoteric arena and look deeply. Who really thinks? By think, I mean original thoughts, thoughts which truly belong to them. The net result is that the noble science of Magick gets buried under dogma. Modern esoterics still make the mistake of following outmoded concepts from the past. For the past hundred years, magicians have been ignoring some of the fundamental principles and techniques of Magick. We find ourselves grappling with outdated conceptions.

Do not make the same mistake. Just because you read a book does not mean the author is correct. Question all, or risk the problems associated with the herd instinct so obvious in today's version of Magick. Learn about Magick. Learn about the planets; learn in your own way because real knowledge gives real power. I will not pretend that it is an easy task but I will promise you that it is well worth the effort. If I ask you, at some future date, to explain the workings of a particular planetary energy, how will you reply? Will you, as most do, quote what someone else said, thought, or wrote about, or will you, as an individual, give me your version?

The greatest barrier to success is the fear of not "belonging." The way of power belongs to life, not to a general trend controlled (and I use the word loosely) by pseudo-Magisters, or subjected to trends or to winds of confusion and disarray. Do not be afraid to drop out of the contemporary magical scene; do not give council to fears of isolation. In order to gain, you must lose; that is, you must learn how to let go of inaccurate and outmoded ideals and concepts.

Remember that there are two sides to the energy of every planet. The first is concerned with what the planet is, the second with what it does. You will find this polarity existing as a constant throughout Magick. First must come force followed by its effect. Every energy type finds fruition here on Earth, and every planet will have its correspondences in physical realities and in other, more abstract, actualities, such as behavior patterns. By looking at, investigating, and categorizing such effects, we are able to learn much about the essential nature of an energy, and from a pragmatic point of view, we are able to recognize the type of energy that corresponds to a particular reality. In other words, first look at an effect, and by contemplation and magical meditation, attempt to discover what caused it in the first place. The planets form a convenient, symbolic means of doing this, but there are other systems you can use as well, notably the Cabbalistic Tree of Life.

Every planet is said to rule a variety of realities which correspond to the nature of the planet. By knowing which planet corresponds to a particular object or situation, we are in a prime position to influence it to our advantage, providing that adequate basic knowledge of magical techniques has been gained. Naturally, it takes a great deal of study before any accurate correspondences can be built up. Acquiring knowledge of the planetary energy takes time. Many useful correspondences are given in this book, but the lists are not exhaustive. They can only function as a useful starting point. Each magician must add to this list.

Correspondences serve two useful purposes. They can be used to provide all manner of stimuli for the mind and they tell us which planet is responsible for any given effect. Never forget that it is the mind that you are dealing with in Magick, and so anything which can assist in concentrating the mind so that it remains on target, so to speak, must be valuable. This is the real secret of correspondences, and, incidentally, why they were guarded jealously by magicians of old.

The correspondences given in this book are correct and have been used successfully. There are other lists: some contain useful correspondences, others are absurd. There are no hard and fast rules which will be instrumental in sorting out the good from the bad; common sense, and personal judgment based on experience are your best guide. In keeping with the essential idea of learning about the nature of a planet and its correspondences, here are some useful ideas about Neptune, Uranus, and Pluto.

Neptune

NEPTUNE **Planetary Glyph** 

Planetary Symbol: A Trident;
Color: Gray;
Metal: None; coral or anything from the sea is useful;
Incense: Ambergris;
Nature of the Planet: Inspiration;
Magical Ritual Uses: Clairvoyance; conscious expansion; crystal reading; divination; dreams; enchantment; Magick in general; mediumship; premonitions; psychic faculties; telepathy; trances; visions. Also helps with confusion of the mind; deception; diseases of which the cause is hard to find; drug addiction; drunkenness; emotional depression; hallucinations; hysteria; inferiority complexes; neurosis; obsessions; paranoia; lack of sleep.

Neptune is the god of the sea. If you really wish to add impetus to a Neptune ritual, use a recording of the sea to help create the right mood or atmosphere. Often, the use of recorded sound, particularly music, is ignored by magicians. This is a pity because sound stimulates the mind, and with the right effects, can make attunement to a particular energy much easier. What could be more pleasant or apt than the sounds of surf acting as a background to ritual work? This is far better than utter silence and, by virtue of correspondence, puts the mind in touch with the ruling planet. (In a similar vein, a ritual of Venus would benefit by the inclusion of the varied sounds of Nature or some music which reminds us of this planet.)

Imagination is a powerful tool. Without it, Magick cannot work. Add inspiration and you have a powerful combination. All imaginative and inspired thoughts belong to Neptune, which is also responsible for daydreaming. Daydreaming is a useful escape, but it can get out of control. Controlled daydreams are another matter because they yield results. Controlled daydreams are known as creative thinking. Do this with your rituals: First think about the rite, turn it over in your mind, allow ideas to flow and pictures to arise in your mind. You will then be surprised at the interesting and practical ideas that spring to mind. The more you become involved in this visionary experience, the easier it will be to improve the ritual and its subsequent effects. I should also mention that a major key to successful rituals lies in seeing a favorable outcome, by using positive creative thinking to maximum effect. This is one use of the potential of Neptune.

One of the worst effects of Neptune is that of escape from reality. This varies from simply avoiding an issue by diverse means to taking drugs. Regardless of what others may think or imply in their writings, drugs have no place in Magick, if only from the fact that there is little control over what happens. With Magick, the potential of the mind is opened in natural ways. With drugs, the mind is wide open to all manner of deceptions. Drugs loosen the mind in the wrong way. Avoid them or those who seek escape in this way.

Perhaps the most popular Neptune effect is that of psychism, in particular clairvoyance. It is a mistake to presume that in order to be an adept, one must develop psychic abilities. Most psychics, that is sensible psychics, almost wish that this gift would go away. You find this strange? I have seen what can happen to a mind when it suddenly sees true. The effect, to say the least, is traumatic and emotionally disturbing. When this happens, the person sees people as they really are: an unpleasant sight far worse than any nightmare. Of course there are those who delight in psychism and use it as an escape from reality, or as a means of impressing others. This is sad and does nothing to explain the real truth about this extension of awareness.

The greatest problem related to Neptune is one of control, learning how to understand what is being seen and more importantly, learning how to turn this off at will. Naturally, there are many degrees of clairvoyance in addition to the total seeing described. These range from mild intuition (sudden hunches) to the ability to see auras or to read minds. It all proves one thing. The mind has many levels of awareness, even if science refuses to recognize this or tries to explain it away. Perhaps one day science will see the truth of Neptune awareness as the reality that it surely is. Until then, a perfectly normal function of the mind will remain buried due to lack of self-discipline and the adherence to silly ideals concerning the unknown or the paranormal.

The main use of Neptune, together with its correspondences, are given at the beginning of this chapter.

Uranus

URANUS — **Planetary Glyph** ♅

Planetary Symbol: The Spinning Cross;
Color: White or electric blue;
Metal: Platinum, uranium (aluminium or zinc may be used);
Incense: Civet;
Nature of the Planet: Sudden Change;
Magical Ritual Uses: Study of astrology; higher intellect; intuition; inventiveness; miracles; Magick and esoterics; sudden promotion; willpower; one's wishes. Also aids convulsions; cramps; disagreements; spasmodic diseases; disruptions; drugless healing; fits; hiccups.

I have spoken often of individuality and its preference over the norm. Uranus is the planet of individuality, a fact that will not remain unnoticed in the coming of the new aeon of Aquarius. You can see Uranian effects beginning to manifest as sudden changes. Look at the way in which technology, especially electronics, is leaping forward at a rate thought impossible just a few years ago. This is typical of Uranus ruled Aquarius. Naturally, there is, and will continue to be, resistance to change by the luddites who prefer the established norm; in fact they are afraid to step outside of it. Uranus is very much the planet of iconoclasm, science, invention, and original thinking. These will make their mark upon society, in spite of the traditionalists. If science is to advance, so, too, must the great science of Magick. This is long overdue, as Magick is in danger of being buried under the religious dogma and collective thought patterns of our times.

Uranus, like Neptune and Pluto, is a magical planet. That is, it has more uses as an arcanum or in an esoteric sense than the others. This is not to say that these planets have no practical use—they do, but in a more abstract way. Among the uses of Uranus are employment of those rare qualities known as intuition, originality, and inventiveness. It is said that nothing is new. When the universe was created, it contained ALL, therefore we are simply rediscovering that which is, and has always been, in existence. Nevertheless, the inventive mind can still further the individual and even the human race. It is the Uranus function which leads to new thought and new ideas. Most of the world's greatest inventions or profound thoughts were not necessarily produced by the establishment-oriented mind. One has only to look at Einstein, who was considered to be a dunce at school, to see that this is true. Inventive, original thought belongs to anyone who chooses to use it. In keeping with the essential idea of Uranus, such thoughts are often brought to the surface by people who could not equate to, or fit in with, the herd instinct's norm. The message, borne out by historical fact, is that if you do not fit, there is hope, providing that you can rechannel your need to be different.

There are many people who are independent or different and find that they are unable to conform to the dictates of contemporary society. It is this difference, this unconventional streak, that sets people apart and breeds potential. There is also stress, as these people seek to bury their individuality, or other problems result from strong-willed awkwardness. Repression is not a realistic solution. The truth is that there is an originality seeking to find expression, and when it does, great minds are born. More to the point, these individuals are free in the truest sense.

Anything way-out, unconventional, rebellious, or eccentric is a sure sign of Uranus working. It is a pity that this energy often seeks to relieve itself in anti-establishment ways rather than expressing the more positive side of true originality. The effect can often be seen in an addiction to cults, especially those which kick against society and religion in a nonproductive way. The real importance of Uranus to the magician is that it can be used to understand SELF in an individual way, and can bestow true originality without the (Piscean) need to join cults, covens, or lodges. Having avoided such practices, the potential for inventive, original thinking is vast. More of the uses and correspondences are given at the beginning of this section.

Pluto

PLUTO — **Planetary Glyph** ♇

Planetary Symbol: The Phoenix;
Color: Ultraviolet (use violet or luminous blue);
Metal: Tungsten (iron may be used);
Incense: Peat moss;
Nature of the Planet: Elimination;
Magical Ritual Uses: Investigations of life after death; discovery (esoteric and Magical secrets); use of hidden forces; legacies; self-purification; spiritual and mental regeneration. Also aids amnesia; sexual problems; guilt complexes; discovering that which is lost; getting rid of that which is unwanted.

Of all the planets, Pluto is perhaps the least understood, despite the fact that it is the most powerful. Pluto is the planet of transmutation, of ultimate change. Uranus is a planet of change because it brings in new ideas. Pluto removes the old in order to make way for something completely different. This is one reason why Pluto is the death planet, for what else is death than a shedding of the old to make way for something better? It is yet another tragedy of humanity that death is regarded with fear. Nothing is final. We should always bear in mind a law of psychics that states that matter can neither be created nor destroyed. This is perfectly true. We cannot destroy anything. It is altered or changed. For example, if you burn a piece of wood it would be wrong to assume that you have destroyed it. The wood has now been converted into light, heat, and ash. The wood does not cease to exist; it has merely changed its state. This illustrates perfectly how Pluto acts.

To return to the idea of death. When you die, you leave behind your physical body because it has literally worn out! In any case, you have decided to leave Earth life in order to move into new pastures. You do not cease to exist. How can you? You are eternal, everlasting, without beginning or end. You are part of creation, an individual who cannot cease to be. This also makes nonsense of dogma such as judgment day and other such rubbish. Such fears have been invented by nonthinkers who simply do not understand how creation works. You cannot condemn a soul to hellfire. Likewise, you cannot punish a creative entity by inflicting karma or any other type of retribution. This simply does not make sense, quite apart from the fact that such ideas contravene cosmic law. Death is not final nor is it to be feared.

Fears, phobias, and similar misconceptions are all part of the negative use of Pluto. They came into being because unscrupulous individuals soon learned that people could be ruled and directed by fear. It is an overemphasis or overuse of Plutonic energy and you can transform it if you want to.

On the positive side, Pluto helps us to rid ourselves of outmoded or undesirable thoughts, beliefs, habits, and actions. With some people, there is an easy shedding of the old and unwanted; with others this is more difficult, sometimes traumatic. It is, however, only difficult because preconditioning is getting in the way. Negative Pluto breeds a sort of selfishness, an inability to let go. What is not realized is that only by letting go can anything better move in. The example of Scrooge should not be overlooked because it shows both sides of Pluto. First the hoarding, then, after exposure to fear, comes realization of the truth, followed by freedom. Remember that we all function like a tube. At one end there is an abundant supply of life energy that we can draw on and use in whatever way we wish; at the other end is physical reality and the effects of this energy. Frequently, because society has taught the doctrine of security in the form of "waste not, want not," or "save for a rainy day," this end of the tube becomes blocked. Energy can no longer flow, therefore better results are difficult, if not impossible, to attain. This is one reason why I have stressed the importance of examining and changing your beliefs. False beliefs block the tube.

Like any blocked tube, there is always the possibility of a pressure build-up or even an explosion. This is one of the major reasons for the many medical complaints today. Most people are functioning like blocked drains! Look at what happens to a human body when, as a result of imbalance or excess, toxins cannot be expelled through the bowels or urinary system. The most obvious example of this is an attack of boils. The eruptions are simply the body's way of dealing with the problem of blockage. In more serious cases we get massive infection because the body simply cannot rid itself of waste products. Now ask yourself what toxins are being produced by the blockages within your mind? More to the point, how are they going to get out?

Fortunately, the body and the mind give ample warning when something is wrong. All one has to do is heed those indications. Common sense care of the body saves much misery. Common sense care of the mind and the emotions is just as important in preventing problems and aiding the built-in Pluto mechanism for waste disposal. All taboos, fears, compulsions, phobias, and bad habits should be looked at seriously. Do you really want these things? Also, when something is about to go out of your life, have the good sense to let it go. Why waste time trying to cling to the past or to some relationship that is no longer valid? The result is bound to be even more distress. All that life is trying to tell you is that, far from taking away some cherished object or personal relationship as a punishment, it is performing the twofold function of clearing away the old in order to let in the new. You can help this process by letting go, taking a positive viewpoint, and then looking to the future.

• • •

Now, what of the future? What does it hold for you? To return to the idea of the tube once more, I, at one end, have supplied ideas and have tried to point out where mistakes are likely to be made. Like the power of life energy, I can do no more than supply impetus, the rest is up to you. I cannot solve your problems; you must do so. At the other end of the tube there is you. What will you do now? Will you read this book and put it on a shelf with other books? Will you presume that it is a little beyond you, or that one day you will give it some serious consideration? Will you dismiss certain parts without thinking in order to retain long-held beliefs that feel comfortable, but may not be valid?

Will you continue as an armchair magician, collecting books and equipment, but not really putting any effort into what has become a hobby? Will you still seek to be initiated or find some comfort in social esoterics? Or will you take the initiative I have tried to give you, push ahead in an individual way, and resolve that no matter what happens, you will succeed? If you do, I will be delighted. Not only will you know that there is more to life than the obvious, you will have what you desire and I will have accomplished my task. You have placed your foot upon the path of magick; the next step is up to you. It may seem a little too simple for some of you, but the truth is always simple. For others it may be too complex. However you view this, it is right and it does work, if you will work with it. You only get out what you put in, results are always proportional to effort—not slavish effort, enjoyable effort. So enjoy your ritual work, take a deep interest in it. It is not a hobby, but a way of life, and a way to real life here and now, so surely it is worth the effort?

Study each chapter over and over again until your Cosmic Sphere and Inner Temple are part of you. "But rather seek ye the kingdom of God; and all these things shall be added unto you" (Luke 12:31). One final piece of advice. The whole point of ritual work is to reeducate your mind so you can create around you all that you wish. With time and patience, rituals may be condensed and equipment may be dispensed with. Eventually, you should be able to perform a ritual in your imagination without any equipment in a matter of seconds. That is the aim and that is true Magick.

Bibliography

Bardon, Franz. *Initiation into Hermetics.* Wuppertal, Germany: Dieter Rüggeberg, 1971.

Bonewits, Isaac. *Real Magic.* York Beach, ME: Samuel Weiser, 1989.

Carroll, Peter J. *Liber Kaos.* York Beach, ME: Samuel Weiser, 1992.

———. *Liber Null & Psychonaut.* York Beach, ME: Samuel Weiser, 1987.

Cooper, Phillip. *The Magickian: A Study in Effective Magick.* York Beach, ME: Samuel Weiser, 1993.

Hill, Napoleon. *Think and Grow Rich.* Hollywood, CA: Wilshire, 1966.

Hine, Phil. *Condensed Chaos.* Tempe, AZ: New Falcon Publications, 1995.

Hone, Margaret. *The Modern Textbook of Astrology.* London: L. N. Fowler, 1951.

Lee, Dave. *Magical Incenses.* Sheffield, England: Revelation 23 Press, 1992.

Ophiel. *The Art and Practice of Getting Material Things through Creative Visualization.* York Beach, ME: Samuel Weiser, 1975.

———. *The Art and Practice of the Occult.* York Beach, ME: Samuel Weiser, 1976 (now out of print).

Regardie, Francis. *The Middle Pillar.* St. Paul, MN: Llewellyn, 1970.

U. D., Frater. *Practical Sigil Magic.* St. Paul, MN: Llewellyn, 1990.

Index